PRAISE FOR TERR

'Intriguing and page-turning

'I really enjoyed this fascinating historical thriller'

'An absorbing novel'

'A marvellous historical suspense that had me
engrossed from the start'

'I read it in one sitting'

'A fabulous page turning, mildly paranormal whodunnit'

'A good read, difficult to put down!'

'Brilliant! Thoroughly enjoyable read'

'I look forward to reading the next in the series'

'A real page turner!'

TERRY LYNN THOMAS grew up in the San Francisco Bay Area, which explains her love of foggy beaches and Gothic mysteries. When her husband promised to buy Terry a horse and the time to write if she moved to Mississippi with him, she jumped at the chance. Although she had written several novels and screenplays prior to 2006, after she relocated to the South she set out to write in earnest and has never looked back.

Terry Lynn writes the Sarah Bennett Mysteries, set on the California coast during the 1940s, which feature a misunderstood medium in love with a spy. *The Drowned Woman* is a recipient of the IndieBRAG Medallion. She also writes the Cat Carlisle Mysteries, set in Britain during World War II. The first book in this series, *The Silent Woman*, came out in April 2018 and has since become a *USA Today* bestseller. When she's not writing, you can find Terry Lynn riding her horse, walking in the woods with her dogs, or visiting old cemeteries in search of story ideas.

Also by Terry Lynn Thomas

The Silent Woman
The Family Secret
The House of Secrets

The Drowned Woman

TERRY LYNN THOMAS

ONE PLACE. MANY STORIES

HQ
An imprint of HarperCollins*Publishers* Ltd
1 London Bridge Street
London SE1 9GF

This paperback edition 2019

First published as *Neptune's Daughter* in 2017
This edition published in Great Britain by
HQ, an imprint of HarperCollins*Publishers* Ltd 2019

A catalogue record for this book is
available from the British Library.

ISBN: 9780008330743

MIX
Paper from
responsible sources
FSC® C007454

This book is produced from independently certified FSC™ paper
to ensure responsible forest management.

For more information visit: www.harpercollins.co.uk/green

Typeset by Palimpsest Book Production Ltd, Falkirk, Stirlingshire
Printed and bound in Great Britain by
CPI Group (UK) Ltd, Melksham, SN12 6TR

In loving memory of Lillian Harper Tombaugh for instilling in me a love of all things Gothic and for her ability to make the ordinary come alive with magic.

Chapter 1

June 10, 1943

Wade Connor's blue Chevy was the only car on the street not covered with a fine patina of dust. I swore under my breath as I stepped off the bus, my document case in one hand, the meager groceries I scrounged with my ration coupons in the other, and headed toward home.

Hoping to slip up to our flat and avoid seeing Wade altogether, I climbed the steps that led to our entryway door and set my bags down, careful not to make too much noise as I reached for my keys. Zeke and I lived above our office, a spacious ground-floor storefront nestled against the hills of Sausalito. My desk and typewriter were tucked into a small office in the back, where I did the transcription work for my boss, Dr Matthew Geisler, who wrote textbooks on paranormal phenomena. Zeke didn't have a title. Instead, he had Wade Connor. Wade worked for the FBI. Zeke worked for Wade on a freelance basis. From my perspective, Wade sent Zeke on secret operations, often putting Zeke in grave danger, and then took the credit for Zeke's heroics. Wade's voice met me as I stepped into the hallway.

'Sarah needs to be told. And she needs a gun, so she can protect herself.' I tiptoed to the door and pressed my ear against it.

'She'll never agree to carry a gun,' Zeke said.

'She will when she finds out what's happened. And you'd better tell her. She'll sense you're keeping something from her, and then she'll wind up in some sort of mess and compromise my entire operation. Be quiet. Someone's there.' The door burst open, and Wade stood in the doorjamb, his eyes ablaze. I raised my hands.

'It's just me.'

Zeke limped to the door. He smiled when he saw me. 'Come in, love. We need to talk.'

I followed them into the office. Once we were all inside, Zeke locked the door and engaged two brand new deadbolts.

'Extra locks?'

'We have a situation.'

The ghost shimmered in the corner of the room, her eyes fixed on me. Wade and Zeke carried on, impervious to her.

'Sarah, are you listening?' Zeke asked.

'Yes,' I said. The ghost smiled and winked at me. I ignored her.

'I want you both out of here.' Wade barked out his orders. 'Go upstairs and pack. Bring enough clothes to stay away for a month or two.'

I stood, ready to lash out at Wade, but one look at Zeke changed my mind. His brow was furrowed with worry. 'What's happened? Where are we going?' I asked.

'Millport,' Zeke said. 'I need to go home.'

'And you're not safe here,' Wade piped in. 'Zeke's going to tell you all about it, once you are on your way.' Wade peered between the blinds again, surveying the street below us, keeping his eyes riveted on the foot traffic as he spoke. 'I'm sorry, Sarah. I don't mean to be short. Zeke will explain everything. I want you two on the road in fifteen minutes. You're in danger. Can you please just go pack?'

'I started to pack for you, but I didn't know what you'd want to bring. Your typewriter is loaded up already. I put the extra ribbons, ink, and a case of paper in the trunk, too. I'll take those.'

Zeke nodded at the sack of groceries I had carried in. 'We can bring them with us. No meat, I suppose?'

'Not a scrap,' I said. 'Do we have gasoline coupons?'

'I've taken care of that,' Wade said.

'Of course you have.' I sighed and left the room.

'Stay away from the windows,' Wade called after me.

With a shaking hand, I unlocked the door to our upstairs flat, frightened now, thanks to Wade Connor. I loved our flat. The bay windows faced the water, angled just enough to the west to allow floods of afternoon sun to fill the room.

The ghost stood before the window now, her image stronger than it was downstairs. She looked like the type of woman who rode horses over tall hedges while perched in a tiny saddle, fearless and bold. Her hair shimmered with golden light. She wore an evening dress of cream silk. It fitted her body and flowed to the floor like liquid pearls.

'Why have you come?' I asked. Although I could see ghosts, most of the time I couldn't hear them. I pointed to a scratch pad which sat on the table near the sofa. 'Can you write your answers?'

She floated over to the tablet in that particular way of ghosts.

'Good. I'm going to pack.' I turned my back on her and headed down the hall toward our bedroom. Zeke's suitcase sat on the floor. Mine lay open on the bed, ready to be filled with the clothes I would need. Something about Wade's manner and the look on Zeke's face struck a chord with me. I realized with a start that I had seen fear, not only in Zeke, but in Wade Connor as well. Urged on by this, I threw clothes into the suitcase without thinking or taking the time to fold them. I jammed the black Lanvin evening gown on top of the pile, not caring that the tiny pleats around the waistline would need to be ironed again – a tedious job that I loathed. I grabbed four sweaters and tossed them on top of the gown.

3

A blast of cold air on the back of my neck told me that my ghost had joined me. She stood by my small writing desk, holding the tablet that I had left for her to write on. When I moved close to her, she disappeared. Her writing was schoolroom perfect. *I am Zeke's sister-in-law, Rachel Caen. You must find the emeralds to discover who killed me.*

Rachel had dumped all the sweaters I had packed onto the bed, and was now replacing them with cotton blouses and light-weight summer clothes. She folded the clothes and placed them in neat stacks inside my case. When everything was properly stowed, she snapped the latches in place with a resounding click. The smile she gave was a sad one. She pointed to the tablet on the table one more time before she disappeared. New handwriting had replaced her prior message. *Be careful.* And just like that, she was gone.

* * *

It was ten-thirty by the time Zeke and I headed north on Highway 1, through the Marin headlands, a picnic basket on the backseat and a sinful amount of five-gallon fuel ration stamps tucked into the glove compartment.

'You've been suspiciously quiet,' Zeke said.

'Tell me about Rachel and the emeralds.'

Startled, Zeke steered the car off the road and parked on the dirt shoulder.

'She came to me.' I bit back the desire to apologize. I had long grown tired of apologizing for something over which I had no control.

'Who—'

'Rachel Caen.' I watched Zeke, trying to gauge his reaction. 'Actually, she came to you. She was in the room with you and Wade when I came home.'

'Oh, just what I need,' Zeke said.

I looked ahead, not quite sure how to respond.

4

'I'm sorry. Truly.' He grabbed my hand. 'I just forget. Your ability to see – it interferes with my logical brain at times.'

'You said no secrets between us, Zeke. I promised you that I wouldn't keep anything back. I am telling you that Rachel came to me.'

'What does she want?'

'She said if I find the emeralds, I will find her killer.'

Seconds ticked past. He didn't speak, and neither did I. Zeke took my hand and kissed it. He handed me the newspaper. 'Read the headline.'

I took the paper from him and scanned the front page. Resting in between the news of the war overseas and the threats of the striking miners, the headline that so worried Zeke screamed,

'FIRE DESTROYS SAN FRANCISCO BARRACKS – ARSON SUSPECTED!'

'I don't understand. What does this have to do with you?'

'The arsonist is one of Hendrik Shrader's men,' Zeke said.

White fear washed over me. A cramp formed in my stomach and my mouth went dry.

Hendrik Shrader – kidnapper, murderer, Nazi sympathizer, and Zeke's mortal enemy.

'I thought he and his collaborators had been arrested.' I would never forget being thrown into the back of Hendrik Shrader's car by one of his henchmen. Hendrik Shrader's threats haunted my dreams to this day.

'When they raided his apartment, he was gone, but they found a piece of paper with our address on it. And I agree with Wade, we'll be safe in Millport. It's a small town. If anyone comes looking for me, I'll soon hear about it. Wade Connor can take care of Hendrik Shrader. Once it's safe, we'll come back and life will return to normal.' Zeke rested his hand on my thigh.

'Will it ever be safe?' I imagined Hendrik Shrader had an army of men, and when one was thwarted, another would step up to take his place.

'Hendrik Shrader isn't my only enemy, Sarah. I have to be diligent. Making enemies like Hendrik Shrader is a component of the life I've chosen to live. I will spend the rest of my life looking over my shoulder, for Hendrik Shrader and others.'

'I admit to being a little afraid,' I said.

'Caution is the operative word,' Zeke said. 'We'll be safe in Millport. It's about time you met my family.'

I believed him. 'Tell me about Rachel. How did she die? Tell me about the emeralds.'

'Rachel is – was – my brother William's wife. My father didn't approve of the match. Rachel didn't come from an influential family. Instead, she pulled herself up by the bootstraps. She was a smart girl. Wanted to be a doctor. Not a nurse, mind you, a doctor. And she probably would have succeeded. We all went to an annual Christmas Eve party at the Winslows'. The Winslows are our closest neighbors. There's a path from our property to theirs by way of a lake that my grandfather built. Rachel left the party early. She brought walking shoes and put them on under her dress.' Zeke laughed and shook his head. 'I remember how she looked, in that long flowing dress, that gorgeous necklace around her neck, those bulky shoes, and her fur coat. She claimed a headache and left the party early. She walked home and disappeared. There was speculation. Many thought she had run away, cracked under the pressure of living in the same house with my father, who was very vocal about his disapproval of William's marriage and Rachel's desire to go to medical school. Her body turned up two weeks later in the lake. She had been drowned; murdered. Rachel's death almost destroyed my brother. He loved his wife very much.'

'And the emeralds?'

'Gone. Disappeared without a trace. My father hired divers to search the lake. He offered a generous reward for their return, but they were never found. They are unusual in that they are round, perfect orbs shaped like pearls, with gold filigree over each stone. My words don't do them justice. They were stunning. Every now and again a journalist rekindles the story, and the speculation starts all over again.'

'I wonder why Rachel came to me now?' I asked.

'Because one of the stones has turned up at a jeweler's in Portland, Oregon.' I took in Zeke's words, playing out in my mind what they meant. 'Surely they can trace the stone?'

'The police are trying. Wade's father, Ken, was the detective on the case. He spent the last three years trying to solve it. He retired last year. I imagine he is still trying to figure out who murdered Rachel. He was very fond of her – we all were. I haven't had much contact with anyone in Millport since I left.'

'What a sad story for Rachel,' I said. 'I think I would have liked her.'

'You would have. Everyone did. William never recovered. That's why he volunteered to go to Germany with me. I made it home. He didn't. Now my father and I hate each other.' Zeke stared at the road ahead, lost in his own thoughts, and didn't speak for a period after. 'I'm glad you're coming with me. I will be better able to face them with you at my side.'

I smiled.

'There's something I've been meaning to discuss with you,' he went on.

'What is it?' I asked, worried now.

'I need you to be careful. I'm not going to tell you to ignore Rachel's ghost because I know you wouldn't listen to me anyway. And don't look at me like that. You know I'm right. But the woman was murdered. All I'm asking is that you take caution. If you think you are coming close to uncovering any information about Rachel's killer, come to me. I will help you. I will listen to you, and I will do whatever you ask. I just need you to be smart. You have a tendency to put yourself right in the middle – enough said. Just promise me you'll be careful. Because I couldn't bear it if something happened to you.'

7

He took my hand and kissed it. We drove like that, hand in hand, connected, each with our own thoughts. We drove along craggy cliffs with the waves pounding beneath us, enjoying the estuaries teaming with wildlife and sea birds and the warm summer sun.

'I should tell you about my family, so you can prepare yourself,' Zeke said. 'My father and I don't get along. I'll leave it at that. I've not seen him in almost four years, so maybe he's changed. I don't know. My brother Simon is a ne'er-do-well. My father spoiled him since the day he was born. He hasn't done a day's work in his life. Father just throws money at him. Simon gambles, and I would tell you that he is just as bad as my father—'

'But?' I asked.

'But he has a wonderful wife, Daphne, who is trying her best to force him to grow up. They have a little boy, Toby, who I haven't seen since he was a baby. My family's mill has always manufactured textiles, namely velvet for curtains and upholstery. They've switched gears since the war and now manufacture silk parachutes. That's about all I know.'

'Did you work at the plant?'

'Of course,' Zeke said. 'We all did – Simon, William, and I. Father demanded it. I returned from Germany in 1939 and moved to San Francisco to work with Wade. He wasn't happy. I have no idea how things are situated now.'

'You haven't missed your family? I never hear you speak of them.'

'I miss Granna and Simon at times, but no, I don't miss my father.' He smiled at me. 'My life is with you. I've moved on.'

We had traveled for three hours when my stomach growled.

'Ready for a picnic?' Zeke asked. He drove off the highway onto a dirt road almost hidden by overgrown shrubs and saplings. He continued about half a mile until we wound up at a gravel parking lot abutting a secluded beach under a steep cliff.

Despite his injured leg and the cane he now used to walk, Zeke carried the hamper with our food. I knew better than to offer to help him, so I picked up the blanket and followed him along the rocky path which led to the beach. Soon we made our encampment and dug into egg salad sandwiches, potato salad, and canned peaches. The cliff provided a shelter against the wind. The crashing waves served as our background music. When we finished eating, we lay side by side on the blanket, basking in the warm sun as seagulls circled overhead. For that brief moment it seemed as though we had no troubles at all.

I kissed him. 'I expected you to forbid me to get involved in Rachel's murder.'

'I don't believe in forbidding. I don't want, nor do I have, that type of control over you. Just stay safe. That's all I ask. If things get dangerous, I'll help you. Will you do that?'

'Yes.' I kissed him again.

* * *

From the beach, we headed inland, away from the brisk sea air and into the blazing summer heat. I dozed in the car for the last two hours of the journey and didn't wake up until we crossed the railroad tracks into Millport. We drove along Main Street, passing a bank, a post office, a pharmacy, a hardware store, a women's beauty shop, and a diner. People milled along the sidewalks. Some window-shopped, some hurried along at a surprising pace, considering the heat waves which shimmered from the ground. Trickles of sweat beaded between my shoulder blades and ran down my back. When I leaned forward in the seat, my blouse stuck to my skin.

We rounded the corner and reached a three-story brick building with a row of police cars parked in front. Zeke drove around the block until we found a place to park under the shade of an oak tree. He rolled up his window and took the keys from the ignition.

'I'm here to fix the business I left unfinished three-and-a-half years ago. After that, we are going to leave and – with luck – never come back.'

We were interrupted by an obnoxious rapping on the driver's side window. Zeke opened the door and got out of the car. The girl who stood outside moved in to hug him, but he managed to turn his back on her as he opened the back door and took his cane out of the back seat. I got out myself, even though I knew that Zeke would have preferred to come around to open the door for me. We moved toward each other and met by the trunk, the woman following at Zeke's heels.

'Hello, Sophie,' Zeke said. 'I'd like you to meet my wife, Sarah. Sarah, Sophie Winslow.' Sophie Winslow reminded me of an elf – a mean elf, but an elf nonetheless. She had a pointed nose and big brown eyes which gazed at me with a fair measure of malice. She wore trousers with sturdy walking shoes. Above the waist, she was dressed in a blouse with a collar made of fine lace. A strand of good pearls encircled her long neck.

'Hello.' She all but ignored me and spoke to Zeke. 'The cane makes you distinguished, darling,' she said.

Zeke moved next to me and enfolded me in the arm that wasn't holding the cane.

'So is this the new wife?' Sophie smiled as she said this, aware of my discomfort and taking pleasure in it. 'She's had her name in all the papers, I hear.'

'Sophie, when are you going to grow up?'

'I am grown up, darling, and if you stick around long enough, you might discover that for yourself.' She changed the subject. 'Daphne's planned a little reception for you tomorrow night. Mother expects you to come to the house at some point for cocktails and gossip. She'll want to get a look at Sarah, of course. They all will.' She faced me. 'You've brought proper clothes?' She didn't give me a chance to answer. 'Never mind. Daphne will help you. She always helps the underdog. God knows, she has a closet full of clothes that she will never wear.'

Sophie didn't give either one of us room to get a word in.

'Okay, darlings. Got to run. Kiss, kiss.' She hurried off, spry and quick, leaving a vacuum of silence in her wake.

'That is Daphne's little sister,' Zeke said, as we walked through the blazing heat. 'Don't mind her. She's a little fool.'

More like a cunning fox. I forced a smile. Zeke held the door for me, and we walked into the police station.

* * *

A dark-haired man with a haggard face and tired eyes waited for us in the lobby. He didn't have a drop of sweat on him, despite the long-sleeved shirt. I didn't notice his missing arm until he pushed away from the wall. The desk sergeant, an older man whose face resembled a bulldog, looked on as Wade Connor's brother and Zeke's childhood friend, Joe, greeted us.

'Welcome, Sarah. I'm so glad to meet you.' Joe Connor had a warm smile and an easygoing way about him.

'How are you holding up?' Zeke asked, as he and Joe shook hands.

'No more boxing for me, but I'm managing. I tell myself to be grateful that I only lost an arm. Others fared much worse, believe me. What happened to the leg?'

'No more boxing for me either. One of your brother's operations went awry.'

'You should get one of those canes with a sword on the inside,' Joe smiled. 'Come on. Let's go to my office so we can talk.'

We followed Joe down a corridor of smoked glass doors with the names etched in gold letters on the outside. We stopped before one that said 'Detective Joseph Connor'.

'Impressive.' Zeke ran his fingers over the gold lettering.

'I'm glad you've come back, Zeke. I'm sorry about Hendrik Shrader and that you and Sarah are in danger, but something's happened ...' Joe hesitated.

'Out with it, Joe. What's he done?'

We followed Joe into his office.

'There have been a series of jewel heists in Millport. The thief – or thieves if you believe some people – targets the Millport elite. Initially the robberies occurred when no one was home. That, among other things, has led us to believe that whoever is doing these robberies is on familiar terms with the victims.'

A large map took up almost an entire wall, complete with pins with red flags, which were stuck in random places.

Joe opened a file cabinet and took out a stack of files. He reached inside one of them and handed Zeke a bunch of photos in various shapes and sizes.

'Things have escalated lately. The burglar is taking more risks and has been entering the houses while people are there, usually while they are sleeping. He climbed up the Donaldsons' drainpipe and stole Mrs Donaldson's jewelry box, right out from under her nose.'

We thumbed through a stack of photographs, all depicting jewelry – diamond necklaces, earrings, bracelets, pearls – and a large quantity of sterling. The burglar had hit the motherload.

I moved over to the map on the wall.

'I've put pins where the robberies have taken place. I was desperate to try something. As you can see, the victims are all concentrated in that eight-mile circumference. This guy is physically fit. He's nimble, which also leads me to believe that he doesn't live here. All the usual suspects enlisted and are no longer in Millport. So we're looking for an outsider, which should help.'

'Are you saying that Millport has a cat burglar?' Zeke said.

'Yes,' Joe said.

'Press?' Zeke asked.

'Haven't gotten a hold of it yet,' Joe said. 'But it's just a matter of time. The victims don't want their names made public, and the various insurance companies are eager to recover the jewels so they don't have to pay the claims. It's a nightmare and of course, no one is happy with my efforts.'

'Surely you don't think my brother has been climbing into people's homes and stealing their valuables?'

'He's recently paid off a large gambling debt. Where did he get the money? He won't tell me. I've asked him repeatedly. There are some who believe that I am not objective because of my connection to your family. You know as well as I do that Simon has been headed for trouble.'

'That doesn't mean he has the emeralds, or that he had anything to do with Rachel's death.'

'I realize that. But an emerald turns up and all of a sudden Simon has the money to pay off his sizable gambling debts. The newspapers haven't yet discovered that one of the emeralds has turned up. But they will. Everyone in town knows. Conclusions have been drawn. I will keep you informed as to what's going on. You're home now. We'll sort this out. As for the other thing, I've spoken to Wade. A few of us in the department know what's going on. If anyone comes after you, we'll soon know about it.'

'Who discovered the emerald in Portland?'

'My father. Since he retired, he's been obsessed with Rachel's case. He claims that he will solve her murder before he dies, and if he doesn't, he'll come back from the grave to see justice done.'

'Do you need my help? If my brother is a suspect …' Zeke didn't finish his sentence.

'As of now, I don't need your help. Since your brother is a potential suspect, your involvement would start speculation and rumor. I can promise to keep you informed, but that's the extent of it. Wade has offered his services in tracing the emerald. That should help, but it's going to take some time.'

'I believe you have something for me?' Zeke asked.

Joe took a black leather case the size of a large book out of his desk drawer.

'I expect you to teach her to be safe with this,' he said as he handed it to Zeke.

'Sarah, this is for you,' Zeke said. He laid the box on the desk and stepped aside. 'Open it.'

I undid the brass latch and lifted the lid of the box. Inside lay a tiny gun made of gleaming silver, with a mother-of-pearl handle. I recoiled.

'What am I going to do with that?' I asked.

'You are going to learn to use it to defend yourself,' Zeke said.

'I will not. I refuse. You know very well that I would never shoot anyone no matter what they were doing,' I said.

Joe Connor intervened on Zeke's behalf. 'Sarah, the men who are after you and Zeke are dangerous. I usually do not condone civilians carrying guns, especially women, but I think in this instance Zeke's right. Just take the gun, Sarah. Let Zeke show you how to use it. Practice a bit. When this man who is after you is back in custody, you can put it away.'

I looked at my husband and his well-intentioned friend. Hendrik Shrader was a dangerous man. I knew that. But the question remained, would I actually be able to shoot him?

'You'd shoot him if he was going to harm you,' Zeke said, as if he could read my mind. 'And I know you'd shoot him if he was going to harm me.'

He was right. With a sinking feeling, I acquiesced.

Chapter 2

'I forgot about this oppressive heat.' Zeke loosened his tie, removed it, and handed it to me. I rolled it up and tucked it into my purse, next to the case which held my gun.

'The mill is about two miles that way,' Zeke pointed as he turned onto a tree-lined dirt road, kicking up dust in our wake. We passed pastures with weather-beaten fences and tall golden grass shimmering in the afternoon heat. Horses grazed here, their coats glistening in the sun. A man on a tractor made tracks through the grass, waving at us as we drove by. We came to a pasture surrounded by a white fence, where four horses grazed. One of the horses, a giant red beast, pricked his ears and raised his head as the car approached.

'Prepare yourself, my love,' he said.

'Oh, come on. It can't be that bad,' I said.

'You've no idea,' he said.

We drove on, following the white fence as it wove around the oak trees. The red horse broke away from the herd and ran toward us, keeping pace with our car. He kicked his heels a few times, before he lost interest in us and ran back to the others.

'That's Seadrift, Daphne's horse,' Zeke said.

We turned into a tree-lined driveway, which wove through a

shady canopy for about a half mile before the house came into view – a two-story structure made of gray stone with a shale roof. A sloping flower bed abutted the driveway. Burgeoning blooms in a riot of color almost shielded the woman who squatted among them. She held a spray can and worked the beds with industry, deadheading blooms, spraying the plant when she finished, and scooting down the row. She had a rhythm and made quick work of the project. I recognized larkspur, foxglove, delphinium, sunflowers, all melded together in a vibrant burst of color.

When Zeke tooted the horn, the woman stood. When she took off her hat, a mass of auburn hair tumbled around her shoulders.

'None of those flowers was here when I left.' He turned off the ignition. 'If we were to stay on this road, we'd run into the stables. All that grassland back there is where we get our hay. What Daphne doesn't use for her horses, we sell.'

'How much property is there?' A fresh batch of sweat pooled between my shoulder blades and started to trickle down my back. I opened the passenger door, but the breeze did little to dispel the heat.

'Three hundred and fifty acres,' Zeke said. 'I wanted to grow grapes for wine and start a vineyard – never mind. Let's go in.'

The door burst open and a ginger-haired boy, who I guessed to be five or six, came tumbling down the stairs and running towards Zeke.

'Uncle Zeke, Uncle Zeke!' The boy launched himself at Zeke, who somehow managed to sweep the child up with one arm, while maintaining hold of his cane.

'Toby!' Zeke spun him around, hiding the pain that I was certain the activity caused. He set the boy down and leaned against the car.

'You must be Sarah,' Daphne said. She wiped her hands on her trousers and held one out for me to shake. She took my hand in a strong grip and shook it, then saw Zeke taking the bags out of the trunk and went to help him.

16

'Give me a hug, brother-in-law,' she said. She and Zeke hugged, and Daphne air-kissed his cheek. 'Simon's at the mill. He asked you to join him as soon as you got here. Why don't you leave the bags, and I'll get Sarah situated.'

'We brought food, too,' I said.

'Perfect,' Daphne said.

'Uncle Zeke, I'm getting a pony.' The boy still clambered over Zeke, who was taking our suitcases, my typewriter, and the box of food out of the trunk.

'And Father?' Zeke asked.

'Running errands today,' Daphne said. An unspoken current passed between my husband and Daphne, words unsaid, but their meaning conveyed nonetheless.

'Toby, your uncle has a sore leg. He's also trying to carry things. Please quit climbing all over him.'

'I can help. Sometimes ponies carry things. I don't know if they carry suitcases, but my pony will do anything I ask,' the boy said.

'That's marvelous, old boy. I think you'd be great on a pony,' Zeke said. He climbed the stone steps and set the box of food next to our suitcases on the front porch. When he walked back down the stairs, Daphne noticed the limp.

'Oh dear,' Daphne said.

'I know,' I answered, speaking just loud enough for her to hear.

The three of us stood for a moment, watching Toby run in circles as he pretended to ride an imaginary pony.

'I should really go to Simon. You don't mind if I leave you?' Zeke asked.

'I'll be fine,' I said.

'I'll show her around,' Daphne said.

'See you soon.' He kissed my cheek, got in the car, and drove away.

'Miss.' The boy came up to me now, as if noticing me for the first time. 'Do you like ponies? I'm getting one of my own.'

'He's not getting one until he can muck out a stall,' Daphne said. 'Toby, say hello to Sarah. She's your aunt.'

Toby skewed up his face, processing this bit of news. In a brilliant flash of understanding, his face broke into a big smile.

'That's super.' He took my hand.

'Sarah is going to be here awhile, darling. Go find Granna, would you? She is waiting to read to you.'

'Yes, ma'am,' the boy said. He waved at me and ran off.

'What a bright child,' I said.

'He's a handful,' Daphne said. 'Would you like to go inside and freshen up, or would you like the quick tour?'

'Should we take the food inside?'

'Don't worry. By the time we get back, Mrs Griswold will have all that sorted out.'

'Tour, please,' I said to Daphne.

'Fabulous.' She hooked her arm in mine. 'We'll start with the gardens.'

* * *

'I try to get out here and tend to these beds myself, but it has been so hot these past few weeks, I've only been able to work in the early morning.'

'How many horses do you have?' We had strolled among the gardens in front of the house, through a rose garden nestled in the middle of a grove of shade trees, and were now sitting on a bench under the gnarled limbs of a majestic oak tree amid ferns, hydrangea, and other shade-loving plants that I did not recognize.

'I have four, all told. Seadrift is my favorite. I bought him when he was a two-year old and broke him myself. I give lessons to the local children.' She stopped as I wiped the sweat which ran down my face. 'Are you okay?'

'I'm just not used to the heat,' I explained. 'Zeke and I live near the bay, so it doesn't get this hot.'

18

'Let's head back,' Daphne said. 'We are desperate for rain. One of these days the sky will break open, and we will get a little relief.'

Daphne pointed out the various plants and trees as we walked.

'It will be cool in the house,' Daphne said. An elderly woman waited for us in the doorway. She wore a lightweight floral housedress – perfect for this scorching heat – with her silvery-blue hair tucked into a chignon at the nape of her neck. Sparkling eyes smiled out of her plump face.

'Welcome, Mrs Caen,' she said.

'Please, call me Sarah.'

We were in a long entry hall. No rug graced the hardwood floor. The whitewashed walls made the room seem cool. Off to the right, a sweeping staircase led the way to the second storey. A cool breeze tickled my bare skin, as though a fan were blowing on us.

'Sarah, meet Mrs Griswold. She takes care of us,' Daphne said.

'And you look like you're about to have a heat stroke,' Mrs Griswold said. 'If you want to take her up, Daphne, I'll bring lemonade.'

'Is there a fan somewhere?' I asked Daphne, after Mrs Griswold had left us.

'No, but it feels like it. It's the design of the house.' We headed up the stairs, taking our time. Daphne kept her eye on me, as if she was afraid I'd keel over. 'We have a cupola on the third floor. If we open the windows up there, and open the front and back door, the heat in the house gets sucked up the stairs. That, plus all the big oaks around the house, gives us shade. Simon has begged his father to install an air-conditioning system, but Will Sr won't hear of it.'

The top of the stairs opened into a sitting area. A picture window overlooked the vast acreage surrounding the house, with a good view of the stables. Four chairs circled a low coffee table, with a sofa positioned under the window. Books and magazines, along with a few picture books and reading primers, were scattered about the room. In the corner, a toy train set waited for Toby.

'What a charming room,' I said.

'Thanks,' Daphne said.

'Did you do the decorating?'

'Yes,' Daphne said. 'I must confess I read lots of design books and magazines. If I were a career woman, I would be an interior decorator. I like studying people and creating their surroundings. Your room is this way.' The hallway had windows along one wall with a narrow staircase in the middle of the landing. 'That staircase leads to the cupola I was telling you about. The view from up there is stunning, but it is as hot as an oven.'

We stopped before a large door, with a heavy brass handle and a skeleton key – also of brass – in the lock. Daphne unlocked the door, handed the key to me, and led me into a spacious sitting room decorated in earth tones. A well-worn rug covered the wood floors, and the French doors, which stood open now, allowed the summer breeze to flow through the room. More French doors opened into the bedroom, which held a four-poster bed set high off the ground. This room also had access to the covered porch.

'I recommend closing the doors and curtains that lead to the porch by ten o'clock in the morning. We've left them open today to air the room. You don't realize how precious this cool air is until afternoon, when the heat can be a bit stifling.' She shut the doors and closed the curtains. 'This was Zeke's room,' Daphne said. 'I've changed it up a bit, painted it, new furniture, curtains and the like.' A small fireplace with a white marble hearth was set in the middle of the wall. On one side, a work table held my typewriter and office supplies, all unpacked and ready for me to use.

Daphne spoke, but her words faded into the background. Above the fireplace hung a portrait of Rachel Caen. She wore the same dress she had on when she appeared before me just a few hours before at our flat in Sausalito. The emeralds sparkled around her neck as though they had a life of their own. Her hair flowed over her shoulders in honey-colored waves. Her expression suggested hidden mirth, as though she thought the whole idea of the portrait a joke. I could not take my eyes away.

'That's my sister-in-law, Rachel. She's gone now, but she was very dear to me. The artist captured her expression so well, it's almost as if Rachel ... Forgive me. I'm getting maudlin.' She wiped her eyes on her sleeve and turned her attention to the small round table with two chairs nestled in the corner, topped with a tablecloth and empty cups and saucers.

'I thought you and Zeke might want coffee in here in the morning.' Daphne wouldn't meet my eyes. She twisted her hair into a bun and surveyed the room. 'Is the room okay? I want you to be comfortable.'

'Everything is perfect,' I said. 'Thanks so much.'

'I'm so envious that you are able to actually have a meaningful job,' Daphne said. 'I would love to work, but Mother forbade me to even think of it as a child. Simon wouldn't care if I got a job, but Will Sr would not approve.'

'Well, I was forced into it,' I said. 'I had to earn my living.'

'I know. I read about you in the papers, starting with Jack Bennett, and then that woman who wanted to kill her husband. Are you a detective, too?'

'Some people say a proper lady's name should appear in the newspaper three times: upon her birth, her marriage and her death.' I met Daphne's gaze head on. 'I have given up any notion of being a proper lady.'

'I like to think you've paved the way, made it a little easier for those who are coming behind you. But enough of that. I want to hear about your job. Surely you don't need to earn your living now?'

'I like to work,' I said.

'Ah, an independent streak.' The smile had come back into Daphne's eyes. 'I'm glad you've come. I hope we shall be great friends.'

'Do you dress for dinner?' I opened the wardrobe. Daphne and I surveyed my meager collection of clothes, which now hung on cedar hangers.

'These are lovely.' She ran her fingers over the fabric of my emerald dress and the black Lanvin gown. 'They'll be perfect for dinner, but if you need anything else, I've got things you can borrow.'

I longed for Daphne to say goodbye and leave me alone, but she didn't leave. Instead, she moved around the room, fluffing pillows, fiddling with the lamps, straightening a picture that didn't need it.

'Sarah, are you and Zeke planning on staying here? Simon thinks Zeke is going to take over the business. He's not very happy that Zeke's come back.'

'Oh, no. We have a business and a home in Sausalito. We just needed to get away. It's a long story, and I think Zeke should be the one to tell you why we came.'

'That's a relief. My husband has the ridiculous idea that Zeke intends on taking over the business and ousting him in the process. Simon's been a bit of a drifter, but he's trying so hard to do the right thing, at least for Toby's sake, if not for mine. I tried to explain that Zeke isn't like that, wouldn't do that. Simon is stubborn, and he's also a bit jealous of Zeke.'

There was a soft rapping at the door.

'Come in,' I said.

A young girl came in carrying a tray.

'Ah, Helen. Lemonade. Good. Sarah, meet Helen Dickenson.' We said our hellos.

'Helen is going to make sure you and Zeke have everything you need. I'll leave you two to get acquainted. See you later,' Daphne said.

'Thanks,' I called after her.

Helen Dickenson was a sturdy girl, with brown eyes and a quiet way about her that I liked right away.

'I've taken a few of your things to be ironed. And I'm quite handy with the comb, miss. I can come back before dinner and fix you up real nice, if you'd like.'

'Thank you, Helen.'

'My room is just next door. If you need me, that's where I'll be, or downstairs in the kitchen. We're all glad that Mr Zeke has come home, miss. I hope you'll be happy here.' With that, she walked down the corridor toward the staircase.

'Oh, but we won't be staying that ...' My words trailed off. Helen had disappeared.

* * *

I lay down on the sofa in the sitting area and soon fell asleep, Rachel Caen's portrait the last thing I saw before my eyes shut. Daphne was right. The afternoon heat was relentless. I woke up groggy, damp with sweat, and parched. The sun had started to set, leaving the room bathed in a soft light that pierced the heavy curtains. The iced lemonade that Helen had brought up earlier had melted. I poured a glass of the watered-down stuff and chugged it, then poured another and sipped. A fan sat in the corner of the room. I propped it up on the desk, turned it on, and headed into the bathroom.

I took a cold bath and had just buttoned my blouse when Zeke came into the bedroom, shutting the door behind him. 'Just me,' Zeke said. 'I've had a—'

Someone banged on the bedroom door.

Was there no privacy to be had in this house? I smoothed my hair and hurried out to meet whoever had come to speak to Zeke.

'Simon, what do you want? If it's about what happened at the

23

mill, now isn't the time.' Zeke's tone was so sharp, I stopped in my tracks.

'No, we are talking about this now,' the other voice said.

I stayed hidden in the bathroom, like a child caught with her hand in the cookie jar, not quite sure if I should make my presence known.

'You seem to think that you can come home, the prodigal son, and waltz into a position of authority at the mill,' Simon said. 'How dare you? You've always been arrogant, but don't you think this is pushing it just a little bit? I've actually done a good job, made a difference to the workers' lives, and have increased the profit margins. Not that Father would notice. He hasn't said a kind word to me in years.'

'Simon, we aren't going to stay here. We have a life in Sausalito, a home, a business.'

'Why should I believe you?' Simon asked.

This had gone far enough. I knocked on the door between the bathroom and bedroom, and opened it, like a lamb going to slaughter.

Zeke leaned on his cane. His eyes flashed with fury as he faced off with his brother. Simon Caen, for his part, seemed just as angry. He shared Zeke's flashing eyes, although his were blue. Both men were tall and lean, but the resemblance ended there. Where Zeke's jaw was determined, Simon's was soft. Where Zeke's eyes held your gaze, never breaking contact, Simon's flitted around. He had the countenance of a spoiled boy, and I judged him to be weak within seconds of laying eyes on him.

'You must be Simon,' I said, forcing a smile.

'So this is the psychic wife,' Simon said. He surveyed me, not bothering to hide his distaste.

'You will address my wife with respect,' Zeke growled.

'Simon, I overheard what you said. We're not staying here. Believe me.'

24

Simon smirked. 'You're up to something, both of you. I would like to know what it is. Why in the hell are you two here?'

Zeke hobbled over to the table and poured himself a glass of watered-down lemonade. He drank it in one gulp.

'I've come to clean up your mess, Simon.'

'I don't have a mess, brother, and if I did, I wouldn't want your help.'

'Are you aware of Millport's resident thief? Ah, I didn't think so. Are you aware that one of Rachel's emeralds has surfaced?'

Simon's face paled.

'They've been reworking the autopsy and other evidence. What do you say about that?' Simon's eyes widened. He opened his mouth and shut it again, without uttering a word. 'And it seems that you've somehow come up with the money to pay off your gambling debts,' Zeke said. 'So how did you get the money?'

'Are you saying that Joe Connor thinks I had something to do with Rachel's … My god, I cannot even fathom this,' Simon said. He started pacing the floor beneath Rachel's picture. The irony of this was not lost on me.

'Where did you get the money?' Zeke asked again.

'None of your business,' Simon snapped. 'I'll discuss it with Joe Connor. That's all you need to know.' He stormed out of the room, slamming the door behind him.

I stood behind Zeke and started to knead the muscles in his shoulders.

'It never will change,' Zeke said. 'Simon doesn't want me here, my father doesn't want me here, and – here's the irony – I don't want to be here.'

I longed for the foggy days, our small, yet comfortable flat, and the day-to-day things that we dealt with at home – finding scrap metal for Jimmy Blithe to take to the corner; Mrs Fields and her cats that were always escaping; the clients who would wander into the office seeking help for small matters, such as lost jewelry or suspicions about wives who had spending problems.

They all appealed to me now. I even missed the neverending noise from the shipyards that were turning out Goliath-like ships at a frightening pace. Now that I had a chance to miss the home we had created together, I realized that our life in Sausalito was very fine indeed.

Zeke stood up, kissed me, and tucked a stray wisp of hair behind my ears, a familiar gesture of endearment that never failed to warm my heart. 'Promise me that you won't let my father upset you. He's an ogre. Prepare yourself for the worst.'

'Surely you know by now that I'm case hardened,' I said.

'Excuse me, miss?' Helen rapped on the door before she opened it. 'Oh, I'm sorry. It's just that I thought you might like me to dress your hair.'

'I'll be back shortly,' Zeke said. He nodded at Helen and left us.

'He's very romantic,' Helen said.

'He is. Now show me what you have in mind.' I took the seat at the vanity.

'Close your eyes,' she said. I did as she requested. She took my silver brush and ran it through my hair in sweeping strokes that lulled me. She parted my hair and started curling and pinning, weaving my hair into loops and curls with the expertise of a professional.

'Okay, I'm finished.'

She handed me a small mirror. I surveyed my hair from the back. Helen had woven my hair into an updo, similar to the style worn by movie stars.

'I can't believe it,' I said.

'You look lovely.' She beamed at me, her cheeks aglow.

'You should be a professional, Helen,' I said.

'No, ma'am. I'm going to be a teacher. But you have such thick hair, it is easy to do up like that.'

I tested it, just to make sure that nothing would fall down during the course of the evening. 'Don't you worry about that, miss,' Helen said. 'It's pinned fast, of that I can assure you.' I dismissed Helen, as she was needed in the kitchen. The sun started to set, so I opened the French doors and ventured onto the veranda, where I had a clear view of the sloping back lawn, followed by miles of the golden grass indigenous to California. In the distance, the stable gleamed white as the horses grazed in the diminishing sunlight. It was still warm out, and the grass smelled sweet. At home in Sausalito the fog would be rolling in. Zeke came out of the bath, damp tendrils of hair curling around his face, and found me sitting at the vanity fidgeting with my pearl necklace.

'You'll break that string of pearls if you keep on like that.' He stood behind me. Our eyes met in the mirror. 'Don't worry. I'll protect you from my father. If you can survive this, you can survive anything.'

'Surely he can't be that bad,' I said.

'We shall defend ourselves, whatever the cost may be.'

And so we headed down to dinner to face Zeke's father, while Zeke quoted Winston Churchill.

Chapter 3

My husband's tension level increased with each step, so by the time we reached the sitting room where everyone had gathered, he was coiled like a panther, ready to spring. The energy flowed off the arm that I held and coursed through me, as we followed the sound of clinking glass and the low murmur of voices. We entered a large room with whitewashed walls, which gave the spacious room a gleaming brightness, accentuated by the large picture window. Through it, the sun set in purple and red streaks. Daphne held a champagne flute while Simon filled it. She gazed at Toby, who was busy with a vast collection of toy soldiers.

'You look gorgeous,' Daphne said, smiling as she walked over to me. 'Pour Sarah champagne, Simon.' She put her arm around me, as though she wanted to tell me a secret. Zeke went over to Simon and busied himself with his own drink.

'I see Helen has done your hair.'

'She also mended my clothes. She is very talented,' I said.

'Helen is a marvel,' Simon said. He handed me a flute full of bubbly liquid, took a sterling silver cigarette case from his pocket, and made a fuss over lighting up. I wanted to step away – I hated cigarette smoke – but was afraid of being rude. He offered the case to me. I shook my head.

'No, thank you,' I said. 'What an interesting lighter.'

'Thanks. Gift from my father.' He handed me the sterling lighter, overlaid with white enamel. On the front a tiny fish under the sea had been painted in remarkable detail. 'It's my lucky charm.'

'Then I'd best give it back to you.' I handed the lighter to him. He tucked it into his pocket, gave me a tight smile, and wandered to the window, where he stood smoking with his back to the room.

'This room is lovely,' I said.

Daphne spoke about her interest in design and her efforts to use light to enhance space. I listened, nodding when I should, or saying, 'Really?' and, 'You don't say,' when a response was required. We carried on this way until an old woman hobbled into the room.

'Granna, look at me! I'm big!' Toby jumped up and flew toward the woman. 'Mamma said we can eat lots of ice cream and cake.'

Granna wore a floor-length skirt twenty-five years out of style, topped with a silk blouse with an elaborate lace collar, held by a cameo at her throat. Toby skipped around her skirts for a moment before he ran back to Zeke, his eyes riveted on Zeke's black cane with the silver lion's head.

'Do you have a sword in there? Some crime fighters have swords in their canes—'

'Not so loud, Toby,' Daphne said. She stood up and went to her son. Soon Daphne, Zeke, and Simon were listening to Toby's tales of heroes with canes.

'That's my fault.' The old woman stood next to me now. 'I'm afraid I let him listen to anything on the radio that he wants, and, well, boys will be boys. Let's sit, shall we?'

We took the two chairs tucked into the far corner, just out of earshot.

Granna said, 'My son – Zeke's father – is a bully and a fool, and I just want to warn you not to expect too much from him.

29

We are glad to have you here, my dear. It is time that Zeke came home. I'm sure that you'll want to stay on permanently after you've had a chance to get the lay of the land, so to speak.'

I was about to tell her that we wouldn't be staying permanently when Mrs Griswold stood in the doorway.

'Dinner, Mrs Griswold?' Daphne asked.

* * *

We followed Mrs Griswold into a dining area positioned inside the alcove created by four windows which formed a good-sized bay window. An octagonal table had been expanded with leaves to accommodate all of us. The open windows provided a pleasant breeze. Outside, the crickets and nocturnal birds serenaded us. Zeke's father already sat at the head of the table, a large glass of amber liquid at his elbow. He surveyed us as we filed in, his eyes mean and hard.

Zeke held my chair out for me.

'This is Sarah, Father.'

'I know who she is,' the man growled at me. 'I followed the trial. I know what you said about that man.'

'I didn't have much choice,' I said.

Mr Caen sipped his drink and watched me over the rim of his glass with watery blue eyes. He had the same features as his sons, intense eyes, and a strong jaw that had once been as determined as Zeke's. Mr Caen was handsome – all of the Caen men were – but the booze was taking its toll. It wouldn't be too long before the skin would hang off the jowls and the eyes would become irreparably clouded.

'You continue to speak to Sarah like that, and we're leaving.' Zeke spoke in that calm-before-the-storm quality that even his father noticed. A hush fell over the room. In the distance, an owl hooted.

'I see someone's knocked you down a peg or two. You're a

30

cripple now. Always knew you'd wind up on the wrong end of someone. Troublemaker, that's what you are.'

'Stop it, William,' Granna snapped, as she sat down. 'Zeke and Sarah made a lot of effort to get here. Let's not chase them off today. Please, everyone, sit. Let's enjoy our meal.'

Mrs Griswold entered the room as if on cue. She carried a pan with roast beef, potatoes, carrots, and peas, which she set on the sideboard. She made quick work of serving us. Soon the room fell silent as we ate.

'The meat shortage hasn't affected us too much,' Daphne said. 'We have a neighbor who raises beef cattle. I give their children riding lessons, and every couple of weeks we get a roast. I grow the vegetables, as you saw earlier.'

'Regular paragon of virtue,' Will Sr said. He turned his focus to Zeke. 'What do you think of the mill? We've made a smooth switch to parachutes. Doing our part for the war.' Will Sr put a piece of beef in his mouth and looked at Zeke.

'Indeed you have. But you need to install an air-conditioner. One of those girls had to go to the hospital today, Father. She had a heat stroke. You need to take care of your people.'

'Too expensive,' Will Sr said.

'Then at least let them work in the evening so as to avoid the heat of the day,' Simon piped in. 'I had to go tell Fred Jones his daughter collapsed on the job because we didn't provide a humane working environment.'

'Enough about the mill,' Will Sr said. 'Let's have some peace while we eat.'

'This is really good,' Toby said. He ate ravenously. If he noticed the rancor among the adults, he didn't let on. 'When I get a pony, I will only feed him grass and alfalfa, maybe some rolled oats, right, Mamma?'

'Yes, sweet pea,' Daphne said.

'Aunt Rachel will lead him while I ride. Just at first. That way Mamma can still teach her lessons and not worry about me.'

All movement in the room stopped. Toby didn't notice. He kept right on talking, despite everyone's attention. I knew that children often saw ghosts, so this revelation from Toby didn't surprise me.

Toby stuffed a huge piece of potato in his mouth.

'Aunt Rachel said—'

The color drained out of Daphne's face. Drops of perspiration broke out on her upper lip.

'Don't talk with your mouth full,' Simon said.

'That's enough,' Will Sr barked.

Toby froze. His eyes widened with fear. He chewed his food and swallowed it with a gulp.

'Get that child out of my sight,' Will Sr said.

Daphne rose and went to Toby.

'Sarah sees her, too. Rachel told me so,' Toby said. His voice quivered. My heart broke for him.

'Come on, love. Grandpa's having one of his spells. I'll bring you some food to your room.'

'Do I still get my cake and ice cream?'

'Of course, extra scoops,' Daphne said.

'That's fine then. Grandpa will be fine tomorrow, right?' Toby said, as he and Daphne walked hand in hand out of the room.

'Did you really have to speak to my son that way?' Simon didn't bother to hide his disgust.

'I wouldn't have to if you would manage your family like a man,' Will Sr said. He stood and filled his glass from the decanter on the sideboard. He sipped his drink and surveyed us. 'You're a sorry lot. I've had enough of this nonsense.'

He tottered out of the room, leaving us all in silence.

'Is this a common occurrence?' Zeke asked.

'What do you care?' Simon didn't bother to hide the sarcasm from his voice. 'You don't have to deal with him day in and day out. He's an irascible fool—'

32

'He's getting worse,' Granna said. She faced Zeke and met his eyes with her shrewd gaze. 'Something's got to be done about him before he drives the mill and this family into the ground.'

'Zeke will fix everything,' Simon said, as he pushed away from the table. 'The prodigal son has come home to save the day. I'm going to bed.'

I was no longer hungry. The bit of roast beef I had taken had turned to sawdust in my mouth. I forced it down with a generous gulp of red wine.

Granna finished her wine and refilled her glass, and then topped off mine.

'Welcome home, Zeke. You've stepped right back into the hornet's nest, haven't you?' Granna held her glass up before she took a big swig.

'Don't you think you should go easy, Granna?' Zeke said.

'I need to drink. It's the only way I can cope.' She winked at Zeke.

We all stood up and filed out of the dining room toward the staircase. 'Would you mind going up alone? I really just want to take a walk,' Zeke said.

'Of course,' I said.

He kissed the back of my neck, a subtle promise that never failed to send shivers up my spine, and left me with Granna.

'Come, dear. I'll walk up with you.'

We walked side by side up the stairs, Granna taking each step slowly.

'Horrible arthritis in my hips,' she was saying. 'I walk three or four miles each day, but the stairs challenge me. Simon offered me one of the cottages on the property, but I can't bear the thought of not being close to Toby.'

'He is a bright child,' I said.

'He's a hellion and I love him to the moon,' Granna said with a twinkle in her eyes. When we reached my room, I found the door locked.

'Oh, no. I don't have a key,' I said.

Granna rapped on the door next to my room. 'Helen? It's Sarah and Granna. Open the door, please.'

We heard footsteps. Helen opened the door. She held a book in one hand. We explained our predicament.

'Just a minute.' She stepped into her room and rejoined us carrying a ring of keys.

'There's dessert for you downstairs, dear,' Granna said. 'Sarah and I need to talk.'

'Yes, ma'am,' she said.

When we were alone, Granna locked her gaze on me.

'Is it true? You've seen Rachel?'

I froze, not sure what to say.

I let my breath out and wondered if I should just confide in Granna right now. Tell her everything.

'You're smart not to trust me yet,' Granna said. 'Best wait until you discover for yourself who your allies are. Do you mind if I come in and sit for a minute?'

She came into the room and took one of the two chairs that faced the sofa. I sat in the other one, awkward and unsure where I stood with this strong woman.

'I've always kept an eye on Zeke and Wade. Those two were trouble since they were children, each of them wanting to save the world and trying to outdo each other in the process. Zeke wrote when he took the job for Jack Bennett. He told me that he had met the girl he was going to marry.' She studied my face. 'You love him. That makes me glad.'

'About Rachel—'

'I am well acquainted with Dr Geisler and his work. It's not every day a prominent psychiatrist walks away from a lucrative practice to study the paranormal. I know what you can do, Sarah.' Her expression was frank and without judgment. 'Rachel came to you with some sort of a task.' She held up her hand. 'No. Please. Let me finish. I know in my heart that Rachel's death wasn't suicide. That poor girl was murdered. She came to you. Did she ask you to find her murderer?'

My breath caught. I nodded, unable to find my voice.

'That's a dangerous undertaking, my dear.'

Granna took a silver flask from the pocket of her skirt and unscrewed the bottle. She offered it to me.

'No thanks,' I said.

'One of the emeralds has turned up. Now Simon is flush with money.' She took a generous swallow from it and tucked it back in her skirt, out of sight.

'How do you know this?'

'I know everything that goes on in this town,' Granna said. 'Does Zeke know that you've seen Rachel's ghost?'

I nodded.

'What an unusual relationship you have. Zeke was always a fair-minded, forward-thinking child. I'm glad to know that he carried that quality into his marriage.' She stood and straightened her skirt. 'Be careful, Sarah. You are treading into dark waters.'

'I know.' My voice came out a whisper.

'You've a friend in me. If I can help, just ask. Good night, my dear. Sleep well.'

Soon Helen came to help me hang my clothes. She offered to brush my hair, but I declined. Instead I crawled into bed, aware of the space next to me where Zeke should have been. The curtain rustled in the breeze as the crickets and frogs made their night noises.

I was sound asleep when I heard footsteps outside my door. I opened my eyes and reached for Zeke, but the space next to me was empty. I got up and padded to the door, flung it open, and stepped out into the corridor. The house had a stillness to it, as if it too had gone to sleep for the night. In the distance a door shut, but other than that, the house was silent. Where was Zeke?

The curtain hanging over the open window at the end of the corridor billowed in the evening breeze. As if on cue, everything went silent. Even the frogs and the crickets ceased their song. I stood in the corridor until one lone frog called and was soon accompanied by the others. An owl hooted, and the nocturnal sounds resumed. I searched for a light switch but couldn't find one. With the moonlight showing me the way, I headed toward the staircase, certain that I would find Zeke in his father's study, poring over papers, or sitting in a chair with a book in his lap.

Goose bumps broke out on my arms. After a second my eyes adjusted to the darkness. Someone was behind me, a presence. 'Who's there?' I turned, but not quick enough. A strong hand connected between my shoulder blades. The hand pushed. I tumbled.

Chapter 4

Doors opened and shut. Voices whispered in the corridor above me, which flooded with light. Footsteps pounded down the stairs.

'Sarah?' Zeke squatted down next to me, wincing as he bent his injured leg.

'Don't move her,' Daphne said.

I convulsed with shivers.

'She's in shock,' Simon said. 'Daphne, brandy and a blanket, please.'

Soon Daphne returned with the blanket. Simon tucked it in around me, his hands gentle and sure, while Zeke cradled my head in his lap. Daphne poured a dollop of brandy into a snifter and handed it to Zeke. He helped me sit up and held the snifter to my lips. I sipped. The brandy went down smooth and hot. Soon the shivering stopped.

Simon examined my ankle. He poked and prodded. 'Does this hurt?'

'No.' My voice came out as a croak. 'I want to try to stand up.' Zeke and Simon helped me to my feet.

'I should fetch a doctor,' Daphne said.

'No.'

Daphne recoiled at my tone. I hadn't meant to snap.

37

'I'll be fine. I just want to get back to bed.'

'If it were broken it would be swollen,' Simon said.

'Are you sure you don't want us to fetch the doctor?' Zeke asked.

'No. Let's wait until tomorrow. I think I'll be fine.'

'Do you have aspirin?' Daphne asked.

'I do,' Zeke said. 'Come on. Let's get you back to bed.' I didn't bother trying to put the weight on my ankle, for that wasn't my problem. My shock didn't come from pain. It came from fear. It came from being pushed down the stairs.

* * *

'Lock the door,' I said to Zeke the minute we were in our room and I was situated on the couch.

He turned the key in the lock and left it there.

'What's the matter? You're scared to death.'

'Someone pushed me,' I said.

'What? Are you sure?'

'Positive.'

'Tell me what happened.' Zeke sat down next to me on the love seat. He reached the afghan that hung over the back and placed it around my shoulders.

'I was going to come and look for you. It was dark. I didn't see anything or hear anything. I sensed someone behind me. I called out to them and was just turning around to see who it was, when they pushed me.'

'There's no way that Jack Bennett knows where you are, Sarah. And I am certain that Hendrik Shrader has no idea where we are. In any event, I'm going to secure the house.'

'I'm coming with you.' I put my feet on the floor and tried to stand. Pain exploded in my ankle. I sat back down. 'Maybe not.'

'I'm locking you in. Don't open the door for anyone but me, okay? I'll be right back.' He left the room. The key turned in the lock, and I sat listening until his footsteps faded away. With great effort and considerable pain, I managed to hobble off to bed. After what seemed like an eternity, Zeke returned.

'All the windows were shut tight and locked. Are you okay?' He locked the door behind him and sat on the bed next to me.

'I'll be fine,' I said.

'I need to ask you some questions while this is fresh in your mind.'

'Okay.'

'Lay back and close your eyes.'

I did as he instructed.

'Was the hand that pushed you that of a man or a woman?'

'I have no idea. They came up behind me, so it's not like I saw them.'

'Okay, think of it this way. Was the hand large or small? Strong? Or soft?' I remembered the feel of the hand between my shoulder blades.

'Strong,' I said, 'but I can't tell the size.'

'Did you smell anything? Cologne, aftershave? Perfume?'

I shook my head. 'No, no smells.'

After he brushed his teeth, Zeke turned off the light and slipped under the covers next to me. When I was cradled in his arms, he said, 'I don't want to think that one of my family members pushed you.'

'What if I surprised the cat burglar?'

'I thought of that, too. If the cat burglar was in the house, I doubt he would take pains to close the window or door behind him. You're going to learn to shoot tomorrow,' Zeke said.

I shivered, but not from the cold.

* * *

Zeke was gone when I awoke to the morning sun beaming into my room. It was already hot, but I welcomed the light of day. Nothing like sunlight to cast away the shadows.

'We'll have to pull the curtains soon, miss,' Helen said. She fussed with my pillows as I tied my dressing gown around my waist. 'Otherwise it will get too hot in here and you'll roast.'

'I don't plan on staying in bed all day,' I said. My ankle didn't hurt as much this morning, and I had no intention of spending my day cooped up in bed. Helen had placed the newspaper on the table, the headlines a brutal reminder of the war: 'RAF, YANKS SMASHING REICH!' The photos beneath the caption depicted a bomb's wreckage and ruin. I flipped through the pages until I came across an ad for Quentin Reynolds' radio piece entitled, 'What Nazis Did to Civilians in Russia.' Underneath that a small headline announced, '17 OUT OF 100 FATHERS MAY BE DRAFTED BEFORE 44.'

'Pretty soon there won't be any men left,' Helen said. She picked up Zeke's shirt and tossed it in the laundry hamper. 'Do you want me to draw you a bath?'

'No,' I said, setting the paper down. 'I'm going to dress and go outside.'

'Do you need me for anything?'

'No, Helen. Thanks for taking such good care of me,' I said.

'I'll go down and get you some coffee and cinnamon rolls. Mrs Griswold's cinnamon rolls will make your ankle feel better,' Helen said. 'I know it sounds crazy, but they have curing abilities. You'll see.'

'Knock, knock.' Daphne breezed into the room, decked out in breeches and tall leather boots. She carried a crystal vase filled with an assortment of flowers I recognized from our tour of the garden. 'These are for you, Sarah. I picked them myself this morning.'

'They're gorgeous. Where in the world did you get that vase?'

'I bought it from an estate sale in Chesterton. It's Waterford, probably late nineteenth century.' She set the vase down on the table next to the breakfast tray and arranged the flowers until they were perfectly symmetrical. 'I scour estate sales and church jumbles. This sort of vase is out of fashion now, but I like it, so to heck with fashion.'

She had used child's marbles in a myriad of colors to secure the stems in the bottom of the vase. I recognized a cat's eye, a couple of clams, peppermint swirls and an abundance of ordinary glass marbles, plain yet brilliant, especially when the sunlight reflected their colors through the cut crystal vase.

'I read about it in one of the women's magazines I subscribe to. Don't tell Toby, a good many of them came from his toy box. By the way, Zeke's downstairs with Simon and an insurance adjuster, who's come about the emeralds.' She said, 'We can listen through the dumbwaiter in your sitting room if you want. Come on.'

I got out of bed, tested my ankle, and discovered it didn't hurt if I was careful. I followed Daphne to the little door that accessed the dumbwaiter. She put her finger over her lips. I nodded in understanding. She raised the door and we both leaned into the shaft, eavesdropping without shame.

'—or anyone in your family have any dealings with any jewelers in Portland, Oregon?'

'Why would we?' Simon's voice floated up to us.

'Never mind the "why,"' the man said. 'I'm asking the questions today. As you know, our company paid a large claim to you when the emeralds were reported missing. Now that one of them has surfaced, surely you can see why my company wants to investigate.'

'But surely you don't think that someone in this family has sold the emeralds to a jeweler in Oregon?' Simon said.

'That's exactly what he thinks,' Zeke said. 'We know that one of the emeralds has turned up in Portland, Oregon. The police have it. If and when it, or any of the other emeralds, are returned to our family, our lawyer will contact you. My family is not in the habit of committing fraud.'

'If the emeralds are recovered, we will expect reimbursement for the claim we paid, Mr Caen.'

'I think you should leave, Mr Spencer. Our lawyers will be in touch.'

'But I—'

'I assure you, you have our full cooperation. I just got into town last night and am still getting familiar with the situation. Thank you, Mr Spencer,' Zeke said. We heard footsteps and a door shutting.

'Zeke certainly knows how to take charge,' Daphne said. 'You love him very much, don't you?'

'Is it that obvious?'

She smiled for a second, before her expression became serious. 'What's wrong, Sarah? Something's bothering you.'

I weighed my words before I spoke. 'Someone pushed me down the stairs last night. I am certain of it, or at least I was certain of it last night. Now I think I'm being fanciful.'

'I can assure you that no one in this family would want to harm you.' She smiled at me.

'Not even Will Sr?'

Daphne's face became serious before she forced a smile. 'I'm so sorry that you had to witness that scene last night. Don't let him bother you. He speaks that way to all of us, except Granna, of course. He's upset because we are about to be invaded. Again.'

'What do you mean?'

'Any minute now the reporters will be at the gate, never mind the police investigation. Will Sr is a fusspot, but he wouldn't hurt a fly.'

Helen came in with a tray laden with a coffee pot and a plate heaped with cinnamon rolls. They smelled divine.

'Join me?' I asked Daphne, as Helen busied herself setting the tray down on the small table.

'No, thanks. I've got to get to the barn. Lessons at nine-thirty.' Daphne walked over to the table to survey the food and coffee. 'Mrs Griswold is a world-class baker. Oh, Helen, make sure that the vase comes directly back to me.'

'Yes, ma'am,' Helen said.

'I'll be off then,' Daphne said. 'Rest well, Sarah.'

Resting well didn't work for me. I had no intention of staying in bed, so I moved over to my desk and transcribed a few of Dr Geisler's handwritten pages. I had just finished proofing my work when the curtains rustled in the breeze, and the sweet smell of the mown grass wafted into the room. I pushed away from the typewriter, ready to be outdoors.

* * *

Downstairs, the curtains were shut, cloaking the foyer and the adjoining rooms in darkness. I didn't hear a sound, nor did I see anyone. I knew Zeke and Simon – and probably Will Sr – were at the mill. I opened the front door and headed down the porch stairs.

I walked down the long driveway, staying in the shade. Seadrift raised his head and nickered at me when I walked past the pasture. In the distance, the roof of the stable peeked out among the trees. Soon I was by myself in a wooded area, the trail covered in dead leaves and lichen. I came to a weathered barn, bleached gray from years of sunlight. Bright green ivy climbed the front and wove through the rafters. A limb had fallen onto the roof and rotted there, long forgotten. I veered left, away from the old building, and toward the sun-dappled lane that led to Millport. I walked along the railroad track, my ankle getting better with every step. By the time I reached the town proper, my injury was all but forgotten.

Recalling Zeke's narrative about the different shops and the people that owned them, I passed the bank, the café, and the general store. I headed for the stationer's. Despite my brand new typewriter, I still liked to write notes longhand. While some women shopped for shoes and hats, my passion lay with fountain pens and thick linen paper.

A delicate bell jingled as I entered the store, a spacious room with high ceilings and white walls, redolent of floor wax and fresh paint. The cool air gave me goose bumps, and I marveled at how a shop like this managed to stay so cool. The influx of workers at the silk mill and the lumber mill was a boon for Millport. The store had a good share of shoppers, evidenced by the long queue at the cash registers, where two clerks, both wearing navy blue aprons with their names embroidered on their chests, rung up sales. Three women stood off to the side of the registers, huddled together, sharing confidences. They all wore hats and gloves, and I chastised myself for leaving the house without at least a pair of gloves. Every now and again, the tallest woman, who I imagined was the leader of the bunch, would raise her head and scan the store, like a buzzard searching for a fresh carcass.

I ignored her and headed for the row of stationery in the back of the shop. The women broke their huddle and stared at me as I walked by, their gazes burning the spot between my shoulder blades. I ignored them and focused on the surprising selection of fine stationery. I chose a thick creamy linen with matching envelopes.

'I can get those for you,' a young girl said. She wore the same apron as the other clerks. Hers had *Betty* emblazoned across the front. 'How many?'

'How about twelve sheets of stationery and eight envelopes.' I could always walk back into town if I needed more. An excuse to get out of the house might turn out to be a blessing. 'I'll just browse for a while.'

'That's fine, miss. I'll have these up at the register for you.' The girl hurried off. I continued to look around the store, meandering full circle back up to the front, where I paused before a glass display of fountain pens. A black lacquer pen with gold overlay held place of pride in the middle of the display, resting atop a blood red leather case.

'It's a beauty, isn't it?' Betty spoke from the other side of the counter. 'It's a 1918 Conklin Crescent. That's real gold on the overlay.'

'May I?' I asked.

'Of course,' Betty said. She opened the case, took out the pen, and handed it to me. My hand slipped as I reached to take it from her, and the pen fell to the floor with a clatter. The cap jumped off and skittered across the floor.

'I'm so sorry,' I said to Betty, as I retrieved the pen, put the cap back on and handed it to her. 'I'm sure it's not damaged, but if it is, I will pay for it.'

Betty's face had gone pale. Tears welled up in her eyes. She stared behind me, terrified.

'You really shouldn't handle such expensive things,' a voice said behind me. 'Clearly that pen is out of your price range. I'd like to know why you even bothered to look at it.' The tall woman with the piercing eyes hovered over me. She had a high forehead and eyebrows drawn into a perfect arch. They gave her a startled expression, counterbalanced by the mean, hard eyes that stared at me with blatant disapproval. A pince-nez hung on a string of seed pearls around her neck. She held it before her eyes and scrutinized me through it.

'That's really none of your business, ma'am,' I said.

'Everything in this town is my business, young lady. You'd do well to remember that. Now who are your people?'

One of her friends approached. She gave me a pitying look as she touched the obnoxious woman's arm. 'Come now. We're going to be late, and I'm starved.'

The woman snorted, gave me a condescending look that said, *'I'll deal with you later,'* and allowed her friend to lead her out of the shop.

'Miss, if you'll step over to the register, I'll just ring you up.' Betty cast her glance at the back of the store where the manager – a mousy-looking woman in an unflattering brown suit – came toward us.

45

'Is there a problem?' the woman asked.

'No, ma'am. I was just looking at this fountain pen, and I dropped it. I'll be glad to pay for any damage.'

A wave of recognition washed over the woman's face.

'Are you Zeke's wife?'

'Yes, I am.'

'Well, welcome to Millport, Mrs Caen,' the woman said. 'We're so pleased that Zeke has come home. I'm sure you'll be happy here.' She took the cap off the pen and examined the nib. 'There's no harm been done to the pen. Don't you worry about it.' I didn't have the heart to tell her we weren't staying.

Betty handed me my package. I paid and headed out of the store, wishing I had asked Betty about the odious woman. *Who are your people? Please.*

* * *

The walk home was a pleasant one. I was becoming accustomed to the heat and, after the chill of the stationer's, welcomed its warmth. This time I took a different path toward the house, through a wooded area, lush with blackberries and wildflowers. As I neared the Caen property, I came across a swing – for Toby, I imagined – hung on the low-lying branch of an oak tree. When I heard the murmur of voices ahead of me, I ducked behind one of the shrubs.

'This is it,' a familiar voice said. 'You can count it. It's all there.'

I peered through the bushes and saw Simon Caen and another man. Simon wore a light blue shirt with the collar unbuttoned and no tie or hat, as if he had come in a hurry. Perspiration soaked his underarms and back. The man who stood opposite Simon wore a suit and a hat. He stood with his hands in his pockets, in a laissez-faire attitude, not a drop of sweat on him. I stood stock still, keeping my eyes riveted on Simon.

'Not so fast,' the man said. 'There's the matter of interest.'

'I've paid your interest,' Simon burst out. 'This is it. I'm finished.'

'No, you're not,' the man said. 'You'll bet, you'll lose, and you'll come crying to me again.'

'I won't,' Simon said. His voice came high-pitched and desperate. 'You stay away from me. I'm finished with you.'

'You'll be back. Guys like you can't quit.'

I never got a look at his face. He walked away, the leaves crunching under his feet. Simon stepped into my view. He stood in the middle of the deserted lane, watching, anguish written in the set of his brow, the pinch of his mouth. Soon he walked toward town, his shoulders hunched, as though he carried the burden of the world there. I made myself wait five minutes before I stepped out into the open. Simon didn't need to know I had seen his business transaction.

* * *

Zeke met me as I came into the house.

'I've got to talk to you,' I said.

'Not now. My father wants us. He's waiting.'

High windows in heavy wood casings took up an entire wall in the study. The burgundy velvet curtains that covered them kept the room so dark that all the lamps had been lit. The effect was grim. Floor-to-ceiling bookcases took up the wall opposite the windows and surrounded a fireplace, over which hung a portrait of a man with the green Caen eyes. Will Sr sat behind a desk the size of a ship, his eyes dancing. He smiled when he saw us and rubbed his hands together.

'Ah, you're here.' A folded document lay before him. He flipped it over, face down on the desk. A gray-haired man with wire-rimmed glasses sat in one of the chairs which faced the desk. He stood up when we walked into the room.

'Good to see you, young man.'

'Sarah, this is Mitchell Springer, our family lawyer,' Will Sr said.

'Nice to meet you,' I said.

Mr Springer gave a nervous cough and wouldn't meet my eyes.

Zeke held the chair next to Mr Springer out for me. After I was seated, he moved a chair from the corner next to mine. He didn't hurry. His movements were slow and deliberate. When we were all seated, Will Sr spoke to Zeke.

'You had no business getting married without my permission.'

Tension radiated from Zeke in waves. Will Sr went on speaking. 'Young lady, I've raised my children to put honor and family first. My children would never accuse the man who raised them of murder. My children would never wind up in court, with their names smeared in the headlines for weeks at a time.'

'There's no need to bring up Sarah's past. You know nothing about it. Her father is a murderer. Why is that Sarah's fault?' Zeke spoke in a calm, measured voice. 'What's that document, father?'

'I'll let Mitchell explain. It's the solution, my boy.'

'Well, Mitchell?' Zeke said.

'You father thought the best thing to do would be – it's the easiest, you know—' Mitchell Springer choked on his own words. He took off his glasses and polished them with the swatch of white linen that protruded from his suit pocket.

Zeke's father picked up the papers on his desk and handed them to Zeke. Zeke stood now and read the papers.

'You prepared annulment papers?'

'You had no business marrying this tart and bringing shame upon this family.' Will Sr didn't even look at me.

Tears welled in my eyes.

'You can go to hell.' Zeke tore the papers in half. He grabbed my hand and stormed out of the office, dragging me behind him. He slammed the door behind us and led me into the foyer.

'I promise that you will never suffer at his hands again.' He hurried up the stairs, half running. His fury overrode any pain from his injured leg. I resisted the urge to follow him. Instead I left him with his rage and burst out of the house, hoping to find a way to deal with my own.

Chapter 5

I stumbled down the stairs and took off running. When my breath shortened and the cramps started, I slowed down to a brisk walk. I kept moving, not paying attention to my surroundings or my destination.

My grief had propelled me all the way to the stable. I stood before it now, gasping for breath, sweat and tears running down my face. The smell of horses and sweet hay filled the air. No wonder Daphne loved being here. I stepped into the shade of the barn, surprised at the welcoming cool air. Daphne stood in front of one of the stalls, holding a shovel. She leaned it against the building and walked toward me.

She stepped into a small room and came back with a canteen. 'You'd better drink some water. You'll get dehydrated if you're not careful.'

I tipped the canteen back and guzzled, not caring that the water dripped down my chin and over the front of my blouse.

'You've had your little meeting with Mr Springer?' Daphne sounded very casual about the whole thing.

'Little meeting? Zeke's father – annulment – I can't even believe it.'

'Come sit.' I followed her into the room. She took a pile of horse blankets off one of two shabby chairs. The walls were covered with ribbons, mostly blue, with an occasional red thrown in. A shelf by the desk held a smattering of trophies. Pictures of young kids – mostly girls – and their horses covered the walls.

Daphne sat down in one of the chairs. I took the other. We sat for a few minutes in comfortable silence. Daphne didn't pry or ask questions as I collected my thoughts.

'So you knew that Will Sr planned to annul our marriage?'

'I did. But I didn't think twice about it. I knew Zeke would blow up, and they would fight. That's what they always do. William goads Zeke, and Zeke falls for it every single time. William used you horribly, though, and I'm sorry for that. Now come and meet my baby. I need to talk to you about something, but this first.'

We walked through the barn and out to the other side pasture area. Four horses grazed on the golden grass. When Daphne whistled, the red horse's head popped up, his ears forward. He took off at a full gallop, his pounding hooves causing the ground to vibrate beneath our feet. Fearless, Daphne hopped over the fence and walked right into the horse's path, not the least bit afraid. He skidded to a stop just as he reached her. She laughed and held out her hand. He dropped his head, submissive. She kissed his nose as he tried to nuzzle her ear. She walked back to the fence with the horse following after her like a well-trained dog.

'Meet Seadrift,' Daphne said.

I held out my hand, uncertain what to say or do around such a magnificent animal. He ignored me.

'He's the finest horse I've ever had,' she said. She rubbed his face for a minute. I waited.

'I know you saw Simon in the woods today.' She didn't look at me as she spoke.

'How—'

'That doesn't matter.'

I had no idea what to say to Daphne. I didn't want to pry into her affairs, nor did I see any reason to lie to her.

'He's forever in debt. You probably surmised he has a gambling problem.' Daphne spoke in a soft voice. Calm now, Seadrift rested his giant head on Daphne's shoulder. As Daphne stroked the whorl on his face, his eyes started to droop. 'I gave him the money and vowed it would be the last time. If he gambles and gets into debt again, I'm leaving and taking Toby with me. I swear.'

'He told the man to stay away from him, if that's any consolation,' I said.

When Daphne stopped petting Seadrift, he opened his eyes and kept them riveted on her as she walked back into the shade of the barn. She sat down on a bale of hay. I sat down next to her.

'They'll stay away as long as Simon doesn't play cards. The problem is I have no intention or desire to police my husband.' Daphne looked at me with sad eyes. 'You and Zeke are so in love. I hope you know how lucky you are. Zeke is a good man. He will never do … never mind.' Daphne wiped the tears from her eyes. 'Never mind that. I just didn't want you to think that I didn't know what Simon had done.' She sighed. 'It's just a matter of time before he does it again. He gets bored here, bored with the mill, his father, bored with me.'

'I'm sorry, Daphne,' I said. I wanted to hug her. I was sorry, for her and for Toby.

'Thanks for listening. Please don't tell Zeke. It's rather embarrassing.'

'I can't promise that,' I said. 'He's my husband, Daphne. We don't keep secrets.'

'Fine. You do what you need to do. I need to get busy.' She stood and brushed the hay off her breeches. She picked up the wheelbarrow and pushed it toward a pile of clean shavings, redolent with pine.

* * *

Back at the house, Zeke rampaged through our bedroom. He rummaged through the drawers and wardrobe, pulling clothes out and tossing them into a pile in the suitcase that lay open on the bed. Helen tried to fold the clothes as Zeke threw them at her, so the result was a small pile of folded clothes, next to an ever-growing pile of T-shirts, pants, and ties.

'What are you doing?' I followed behind him, taking the clothes that he tossed on the bed, still on their hanger, and putting them back in the closet. Helen folded clothes as fast as she could, not looking at either one of us.

'We are leaving,' Zeke said. 'I've had it with my father. Damn the mill, damn Simon, and damn him. I've reached the limit of my ability to cope.' He looked at the white shirts he held in his hands, handed them to me, and walked to the window. I hung the shirts up and went over to Helen.

'Come and get us in time to dress for dinner,' I said in a soft voice. Relief flooded her face.

She ran out of the room before either one of us changed our minds.

I fussed with the pile of clothes on the bed while Zeke stared out the window.

'You don't think we should leave?' he asked.

'I don't think you should run away.' I went to him and took his hands in mine. 'You'll never forgive yourself, and you know it. Don't you think you should face your father?' I realized as I uttered the words that I needed to face Zeke's father, too. I vowed then and there that Will Sr would never again make me cry.

'We can face him together,' I said. 'If we need to retreat, we can do so together.'

'Something's bothering you.' Zeke met my eyes. 'What did you want to talk to me about?'

'I walked into town today,' I said. 'On the way home, I saw Simon and another man. I hid and spied on them. Simon gave

53

the man a packet of money. He told the man that he was finished with him and to stay away from him.'

I wanted to tell him about the lost love between Simon and Daphne, and the sadness in her eyes when she spoke of it, but Zeke chose this moment to kiss me. Daphne faded from my mind.

* * *

The mellow afternoon sun filtered through the leaves and cast patterns on the hardwood floor in the bedroom. Content, I lay in bed next to a sleeping Zeke, as the shadows danced in the afternoon breeze.

'Miss.' Helen knocked softly.

'Just a second,' I said.

Next to me, Zeke stirred.

'Time to get up,' I said, belting my dressing gown around my waist as I slipped into the sitting room, pulling the bedroom door shut behind me.

'Here's some ice water and lemonade. It's hotter than blazes this afternoon.' Helen set the tray down and locked the door, leaving the key in the lock. 'Shall I draw you a nice, cool bath?'

'Yes,' I said.

Helen glanced at the closed door, a knowing look on her face. 'Did you want to wear the black dress, with the pearls?'

'I was thinking the emerald dress tonight,' I said, knowing that my husband favored that dress, and I liked the look in his eyes when he saw me in it. Zeke came into the room, buttoning the shirt he had worn earlier.

'I'll bathe after you,' he said. 'I'll be back in a few minutes.'

'Your shirt's buttoned crooked, and you're barefoot. Where are you going?'

'To see Granna.' He shut the door behind him before I could inquire further.

I soaked in bathwater scented with some exotic spice that

54

Daphne had left for me. An hour later, I sipped cold water from a crystal glass as Helen brushed my hair. She swept it up and secured it in place with the silver combs.

'I'm glad you don't wear it short,' she said.

'It's easier this way.' I examined my reflection in the mirror. 'I can pin it up. If I left it short, it would just frizz up.'

'Most women would give their eye teeth for hair like yours,' Helen said. She cleared the hairbrush and extra pins from my vanity and placed them in the small dish that lay there. 'You'll have fun tonight,' she said.

We were interrupted when the door opened and Zeke came in. He winked at me, smiled at Helen, and went into our bedroom to dress for dinner.

I dismissed Helen. She hurried down to the kitchen for dinner with Mrs Griswold, after which she would spend a quiet evening reading. I told her not to wait up for me, and she was grateful. I was sitting on the sofa, reading a magazine, when Daphne knocked on my door.

'Hello. I came in to see—' She stopped. 'That dress is fabulous. You look absolutely stunning.' She laughed. 'And to think I was coming in to see if you needed a loan of clothes, shoes or stockings. You'll put us all to shame. The green reminds me of the Caen eyes. I did bring you this,' she said, holding up a lightweight shawl embroidered in jewel tones with silken thread. 'It can get chilly in the house, especially of an evening.' She fiddled with the shawl for a moment. 'Sarah, I wanted to tell you not to let my mother bother you this evening. She can act like an ogre, so I'm apologizing for her in advance.'

Why does everyone feel compelled to apologize for their parents?

'Oh, I'm sure it will be fine.'

Daphne shook her head. 'You don't understand. She really is rather brutal. I just, well – I am giving you permission to be rude right back to her. That's the only way to deal with her. If you don't stick up for yourself, she'll tromp all over you.'

She kissed my cheek, passing Zeke on her way out the door. 'You need shoes, darling,' she teased him. 'And a coat.'

'Get out of here.' His smile took the sting out of his words.

'See you downstairs,' she said, as she shut the door behind her. Zeke stared at me, his eyes sparkling. I twirled.

'Who did your hair like that? You look like a movie star.'

I caught Zeke's reflection in the mirror. 'What are you holding behind your back?'

'A present for my beautiful wife.' He came close and wrapped his arm around me. He held out a blue jewelry box with a brass catch on the front. I released it, and inside, tucked in a nest of white silk, under the emblazoned words *Tiffany and Company – New York*, lay two perfect pearls, each with a cluster of diamonds underneath. I gasped.

'They're beautiful.'

'Put them on,' he said.

As I took the earrings out of their box and put them on, Zeke came up behind me. 'Daphne gave me permission to be rude to her mother,' I said. He met my eyes in the mirror, the beginning of a smile on his face.

'What's so funny? Are you saying that Daphne's mother is really that horrid?'

'Oh, she's horrid, all right. It's just the idea of you being rude to her, or anyone for that manner. You haven't got rudeness in you, my love. You are social graces personified.'

Nervous now, I broke away from his embrace. 'Come on, let's go down. I'm thirsty.'

The murmur of voices echoed into the hallway as Zeke and I walked down the stairs.

'Don't be nervous, love.'

'I'm not,' I said.

'Part of me wants to walk right past the company and go eat at the all-night diner in town,' Zeke said.

'Part of me would be happy to accompany you.'

The crowd fell silent for just a second when Zeke and I stood in the doorway. Granna sat down in a chair, bouncing Toby on her lap. Simon and Joe Connor stood in the corner of the room. Simon had taken to ignoring me. He did so now. Daphne spoke with Will Sr, Sophie, and another woman with auburn hair interlaced with gray.

'Oh, no,' I uttered.

Mrs Winslow did well at hiding her surprise at seeing me with Zeke. She didn't mention our run-in at the stationer's, thank goodness.

'Come in, you two. The champagne's just cold.' Daphne came toward us with flutes of golden liquid, their tiny bubbles floating to the surface. I took mine and sipped.

'Sarah, I think you know most everyone.' Daphne took my arm and led me toward her mother. 'This is my mother, Arliss Winslow. Mother, this is Zeke's wife, Sarah. We are going to be great friends.'

'That's nice,' Mrs Winslow said. She didn't bother to excuse herself. She just walked away without a backward glance.

Daphne faced me, her eyes full of concern. 'I told you. Please don't take anything she says or does personally.'

Mrs Griswold supervised the two young women who had been hired for the evening to serve dinner. They wore ill-fitting black uniforms that smelled of mothballs, left over from the days when dining formally was the norm. The sideboard had been cleared of its usual bric-a-brac and now held several trivets, in anticipation of hot plates that would be served. Daphne and I meandered over to Zeke, who sat next to Granna and Toby. Toby regaled Zeke with some sort of story. He gestured while he spoke, his face serious, while Zeke did his best not to laugh. I smiled at them and sipped champagne. Daphne watched her son with adoring eyes. Granna, who had dressed for the occasion in the same long black gown and cameo broach as the night before, looked as though she had stepped out of a Brontë novel. All that was missing were the windswept moors. I had no idea how she managed such a dress in this heat. She watched me, concern etched into her eyes. She moved close to me and took my hand.

'Don't let her bother you, dear. She's a beast and everyone knows it. If she gives you any difficulty, come to me and I'll take care of it.'

Joe and Simon were tucked into the corner, their heads bent together, engaged in a serious conversation. Granna she tickled Toby's ribs. He burst into gleeful laughter.

My head started to pound, the inchoate sign of the impending headaches that I got during times of stress. I took the warning sign as a blessing, set my champagne down, and hurried up to my room for aspirin. I had just taken the pills, and had paused before Rachel's picture, when Arliss Winslow's voice startled me.

'What do you want?' I didn't bother to act polite.

'I've something to say to you, and you'd do well to listen.'

'Since you're blocking the door, I don't really have a choice, do I?'

'I suggest you wipe that smug look off your face, young lady,' Mrs Winslow said.

'What can I do for your Mrs Winslow? Say your piece and leave me alone.'

'Fine.' She fiddled with the string of jade that hung around her neck. 'I intend for Sophie to marry Zeke. I know that Mr Caen presented you with an annulment. I suggest you convince your husband that the best thing to do would be for you to sign it.'

'Get out,' I said.

'I will win on this, Ms Bennett. I have Will Sr's support. You don't stand a chance.'

'If you don't leave, I'll get my husband. You can tell him of your little plan.'

Arliss didn't hear me. She stared at Rachel's picture. 'Oh, my god.' She almost choked on her words. The color drained from her face. She sat down on the couch, as if her knees could no longer hold her.

'Mrs Winslow, are you alright? Should I get Daphne?' I hurried over and placed a hand on her shoulder.

'Don't touch me.' She brushed my hand away and met my eyes.

I stepped away, unsettled by this sudden change in her personality.

Behind Arliss Winslow, the notebook which lay on my desk opened. The pages fanned out, as though someone were perusing them. Rachel appeared, a diaphanous outline in the dim light of my room. She had opened the book and was rifling through it. Arliss turned just then. She stiffened.

'Rachel?' She choked on her own words.

I strode to the table and read the words that Rachel had left in my notebook. *She knows.*

I turned to face Arliss.

'What do you know? You need to tell me!' My words cut through Arliss's fear, strong and sure.

She got up, her face pale and covered with a sheen of sweat. She staggered a bit, but somehow managed to make her way out of the room.

More writing appeared in the notebook, and Rachel, with the kiss of a summer breeze, bade me follow her. She shimmered to the bedroom door and summoned me with the crook of her finger. I followed.

Rachel moved down the stairs and into a warren of windowless hallways. I followed her, trusting that she had some purpose in mind. Arliss Winslow might know who killed Rachel and who stole the emeralds, but I was certain that Arliss Winslow would not share that information with me.

'Come.' Rachel's voice was an icy breath in the hot summer night.

I had been following like a blind person, unfamiliar with my surroundings, down dark corridors with no windows to light the way. God help me, I was following a ghost. When the absurdity of my situation hit me, I decided to toss it in and head back to the party. I had no business in this part of the house, and I could not explain my presence here, should I need to. But then I saw light spilling under a closed door in the hallway. I stopped. Stood frozen. In the distance I heard laughter and footsteps. Rachel disappeared into the room. When the footsteps passed, I opened the door from which the light seeped, stepped into the room, and closed the door behind me.

A lamp had been left on. It provided a small glow of light that left the rest of the room in shadows. A soiled blue shirt lay in a heap on the floor, next to a pair of trousers. A red tie had been taken off and tossed over the back of a chair. A bed pillow and a gray army-issue blanket lay in a pile on the leather sofa. I recognized the familiar red pack of Dunhill cigarettes and the enamel lighter with the hand-painted fish that lay on the coffee table next to an ashtray filled with butts.

Simon's clothes. Simon's mess. Simon's room.

Like all the rooms on this side of the house, a bay window took up the biggest part of one wall. I imagine it, too, had French doors that led out into the terrace. Now, the alcove was covered by the heavy brocade curtain. A desk sat in front of the window, facing the room. Rachel's ghost stood near Simon's desk, her arms out to her side, a look of desperation on her face.

'What do you want me to do?'

Her lips moved, but I couldn't hear her. She pointed at the desk.

The room grew cold. My breath came like dragon's fire. I shivered and moved toward Rachel.

'You want me to search the desk?'

Rachel nodded.

'What am I looking for?' I whispered.

Her form became more solid, the expression on her face clear. I was overcome with a feeling of desperate sadness.

'The emeralds?' I whispered.

She nodded. Tears welled in her ghost eyes. She wiped them away and disappeared. Rachel wanted me to find the emeralds. What if they were in Simon's desk, hidden in some secret compartment? Would that mean that Simon killed Rachel?

The brocade curtain moved just as I reached the desk. I stopped in my tracks and listened.

Nothing.

A brass letter opener lay on top of the desk. I held it in my hand – a quick weapon at the ready – stepped around the desk, and whipped the brocade curtain open with one sweeping gesture.

The night air, sweetened by the jasmine that grew on the trellises that lined the back of the house, rushed over me. The frogs silenced for a moment, as if waiting to see what I would do. I slid the curtains back to their shut position. I stood behind the desk now, my back to the window. I opened the top drawer and saw the usual junk, postage stamps, an opened pack of cigarettes, a few envelopes, unopened, addressed to Simon. There were two drawers on either side of the desk. One of them held a stack of folders. I didn't know what Rachel's ghost wanted. There wasn't anything in this desk. If Simon were going to hide something, surely he wouldn't be so stupid as to hide the emeralds in the desk, where anyone could find them.

I opened the second drawer. A rucksack made of canvas had been jammed into the back of it. I picked it up and set it on the desk.

'What are you doing in here?' Zeke startled me. 'What've you got there?'

His eyes were riveted on the bundle on the desk. He undid the cotton cord that held it together, so the fabric fell away.

Two silver candelabras, several strings of pearls, a diamond bracelet, and a myriad of other jewelry – necklaces, earrings, brooches, and bracelets – glistened under the soft lamp on the desk. We had found the cat burglar. At the very least, we had found the burglar's loot.

Chapter 6

'Good god,' Zeke said.

'Oh,' I said at the same time.

'Simon.' Zeke ran his hand over his face, pinching the bridge of his nose, as if to stave off a headache. He took a deep breath and met my gaze. 'Is Joe still here?'

'I think so,' I said.

'Stay here. I'm going to get him.' Zeke slipped away, leaving me with the bag of loot. I opened it and rummaged through the jewelry and silver. Some instinct made me reach into the bag until I found a black felt bag. I untied the silk string that held it fast and dumped two emeralds in my hand.

They looked like small marbles, dense and alive and full of secrets. I had never seen emeralds that weren't cut into facets before. These were heavy with a color so rich it stunned the eyes.

When Joe and Zeke burst through the door, I looked up at them, the emeralds in my open palm.

Zeke's eyes locked on the stones. He was by my side in two steps.

'Where did you find those?' He put the emeralds back into the tiny felt bag.

'In this bag at the bottom.' I nodded at the rucksack.

62

'Give the emeralds to me, please.' Joe held out his hand. Zeke gave him the emeralds.

'Did you touch anything?' Joe asked.

'I may have touched some of the items in the bag,' I said.

'That's okay,' Joe said. 'We'll take your fingerprints at the station tomorrow, so we can eliminate you. Zeke, we'll take yours, too.' He opened the bag, surveying what it held. 'These are all things that were recently stolen. Sarah, you say you found them in the desk?'

'Yes,' I said. 'The canvas bag was in that drawer.'

'And what were you doing in here?' Joe asked.

I tried to speak but stumbled over my words.

'What were you looking for? Never mind that. I'll deal with you later. I need to see Simon. Meanwhile, Sarah, keep your nose out of this. I'm not kidding. And do not breathe a word of this to anyone. Zeke, I expect you to get a handle on your wife.'

'Fine,' Zeke said.

'What the hell are you doing in my room?' Simon bellowed. He stood in the doorway, a bottle of champagne in one hand, a lit cigarette in the other.

'He's drunk,' Joe said under his breath.

'You'd better come in here,' Zeke said, 'and shut the door behind you.'

Simon stepped into the room and had almost shut the door when Will Sr burst in behind him.

'You're both being rude. We've dinner guests—'

Alcohol fumes came off the two men in waves. At least Will Sr was steady on his feet. He pushed Simon aside and walked to the desk. He started to pick up one of the necklaces, but Joe pushed his hand away.

'Please don't touch that, sir. It's evidence.'

'Evidence of what?' Will Sr asked.

Joe shook his head. I didn't envy his position. 'This is stolen property. We found it in Simon's desk,' Zeke said.

'I blame you for this,' Will Sr pointed at me.

'Do not take that tone with my wife.' Zeke spoke through clenched teeth.

'I'll take whatever tone I choose,' Will Sr said. 'This is my house, and you brought this little tart here to make trouble for all of us. I swear, I ought to throttle you.'

Zeke leaned his cane against the desk, freeing both of his hands. He met his father's eyes. The room was silent. Joe stepped back. He grabbed my elbow and pulled me away, too. Simon didn't say a word. He sat on the couch watching Zeke and his father square off. Zeke would make quick work of him, cane or no cane, in a physical fight. Will Sr took a deep breath. He shook his head and moved away from Zeke.

'I don't want any part of this. Simon, if you're in trouble, you'll have to get yourself out of it. I'm going back to my guests.' He lumbered out the door, slamming it shut behind him so hard that a picture fell off the wall.

'Simon, what is this?' Joe pointed at the pile of stolen goods.

'I swear I've never seen it,' Simon said.

'Is this how you've been paying your gambling debts? Are you the cat burglar?' Zeke couldn't keep the disdain from his voice.

'My gambling debts are none of your business,' Simon said. He stood and set the champagne bottle on the coffee table. He surveyed the stolen items. 'I've never seen this stuff before.'

'I should arrest you, but I'm not going to because I believe that if you did steal these things, you would not be stupid enough to leave them in your desk,' Joe said. 'You need to come down to the station tomorrow. I'll take your statement and your finger-prints. If you're lucky, I won't have to arrest you. If you don't show, I'll find you and lock you up myself.' He picked up the phone and asked the operator to put him through to the police.

* * *

64

Joe had somehow managed to keep our discovery a secret from the dinner guests. We all knew that by morning the entire town would know what we had found in Simon's desk. Joe arranged for a detective to come and take the stolen items to the police station, where they would be catalogued as evidence and eventually returned to their rightful owners. Zeke and I slipped out the French doors and drove into town, grabbing a hamburger at the only late-night diner in Millport.

We didn't speak of what we had found in Simon's desk – the jewels stolen by the cat burglar and the emeralds stolen from Rachel Caen's body. But the implication of Simon's involvement in Rachel's murder hung over us like a dark cloud, a portent of what was to come.

Chapter 7

I woke up to bright sunlight streaming in my bedroom. The spot where Zeke should have slept lay empty, the sheets in a mess where he had lain. The faint scent of him lingered. A piece of my new stationery, folded in half with my name scrawled across the front, rested on the pillow.

My love, Went to the mill. We can check into a hotel if you wish. Will discuss this afternoon. Z

'Good morning, miss.' Helen moved through the doorway, holding a tray loaded with food.

'Put it out there. Be with you in a moment,' I said. I stood and wrapped the aqua silk dressing gown – a wedding present from Zeke – around my naked body, savoring the feel of the silk against my skin.

In the sitting room, Rachel's portrait looked down at me, a reminder of the events of the previous night. I ignored it and watched Helen as she fussed with a carafe of orange juice. The tray was laden with toast, bacon, eggs, and a large coffee pot.

'Bacon. Oh, how I have missed meat.'

'I've heard there isn't any to be had in the City,' Helen said. She poured me coffee and handed me the cup and saucer.

'I don't suppose you've heard about what happened last night.' I sipped my coffee, not meeting Helen's eyes.

'Everyone's talking about it downstairs,' Helen said. 'Mr William is furious with Mr Zeke, and with you, miss, if you don't mind me saying so. He says you had no business going into Simon's room.'

'I couldn't help it. I got lost on the way to the kitchen.'

'But he didn't steal those things, miss. I'm certain of it. He wouldn't have done.' Her eyes glistened with unshed tears.

'You're fond of Simon?'

'He's been a good friend,' she said. 'And he wouldn't do anything that would take him away from Toby. He loves that boy more than—' Helen held her tongue at the last minute. 'Mrs Griswold doesn't know that I dust his room and press his clothes. She wouldn't approve, with Simon being a married man. But he's so kind and generous. He knows that I need to save money, to make a better life for myself. I'm saving for school. I want to be a teacher. Simon – Mr Simon – gave me twenty dollars at Christmas.' She plumped the cushions on the chairs and picked up my clothes from the evening before.

'I'll just take these and press them for you. Will you be needing anything else?'

The stack of Dr Geisler's handwritten notes taunted me. I did have work to do. 'No. What are you going to do today?'

She gave me a startled look as though she were surprised that I would ask such a question, as though she were surprised that I cared.

'After I tend to this lot—' she held up the clothes piled over her arm '—I was going to help my dad at home. We have a victory garden, and the tomatoes are coming on. I told him I would help with the picking. If that's okay?'

'Of course,' I said.

* * *

67

I worked all morning, taking comfort in the sound of my type-writer keys clacking on the platen. The hours flew by. Daphne surprised me when she came in at one o'clock, still wearing tight breeches and high leather boots. Several dresses hung over her arm.

'Am I disturbing you? I knocked, but you didn't hear.' She laid the dresses over the back of the couch.

'Not at all.' I put the typed pages into an envelope to be mailed to Dr Geisler, stuffed everything else into the top drawer of the desk and stood, stretching my neck. Toby, also dressed in riding clothes, burst into the room. He came to an abrupt halt when his eyes lit on the typewriter. His mouth opened in shock. He looked at his mother, looked at me, and moved toward my desk. When he got close, he stopped and stared.

'May I please touch it?'

'Of course,' I said.

'Thank you,' he said. He rubbed the typewriting machine as though it were a puppy or a horse. 'I like the sound of the keys,' Toby said. He skipped over to Rachel's portrait and stared up at it for a second, while Daphne and I watched. 'Rachel says to remember your promise, Aunt Sarah.'

I dropped my coffee cup. A brown stain bloomed on the clean carpet.

'Toby, stop talking nonsense,' Daphne snapped.

'I'm not talking nonsense,' the little boy said. 'I mucked out Seadrift's stall all by myself and now I can get a pony.'

'Sweetheart.' Daphne moved over to Toby and squatted down in front of him. 'I think it's time for you to go change your clothes and wash up. Lunch will be ready soon.'

'That's good because I'm really hungry. Do you think there will be any cookies for me?'

'I bet there will be. Now run along.'

Toby kissed his mother's cheek, waved at me, and ran out of the room.

'That's the kind of thing that will start the gossip. Granna tells him ghost stories. She's very good at it. Scares the child half to death, but he loves them.'

'Toby's got a vivid imagination.'

'Oh, that he does.' She stood with her back to me, plucking the dead leaves and brown blooms off the flower arrangement she had given me.

I put the envelope for Dr Geisler into my document case and covered my typewriter.

'Do you like your work? I'm surprised Zeke doesn't want you to stay home – no, I take that back. Zeke is the type of husband who would give his wife free rein.' She sighed. 'You don't know how lucky you are.'

'Surely Simon—'

'Oh, no, Simon lets me have my freedom. It's my mother. She placed so many expectations on Sophie and me. She's managed to suffocate both of us. I manage somehow. Thank god for Seadrift and Toby, of course, but my poor sister is bored. She's desperate to do something with her life, get out of Millport, go to college, but my mother won't let her.' She walked over to the dresses and picked up a floor-length, midnight-blue velvet with a plunging neckline. 'I'm sure my mother will be formally dressed this evening, so I brought some dresses for you.'

'I did bring one floor-length gown,' I said, as I opened the wardrobe and took out my best dress.

'Oh, that's lovely.' Daphne fingered the heavy black silk. 'It will look beautiful with your pearls.'

'Excuse me.' Helen knocked on the door and stuck her head in. 'Mrs Griswold sent me to tell you that sandwiches and lemonade will be served on the patio in fifteen minutes.'

'Thank you, Helen,' Daphne said. 'Would you please tell Granna to have Toby ready? I know the child is starved. He really did work hard this morning.'

'Yes, ma'am,' Helen said.

'Helen, I've spilled coffee on this carpet. If you'll bring me some damp rags, I'll clean it.'

'Don't worry, miss. I'll take care of it,' Helen said.

When Daphne and I were alone once again, she said, 'Will Sr won't be eating with us, Sarah. If it makes you feel better, I promise not to leave you alone with him.'

'He was so angry last night,' I said.

'William reminds me of a volcano,' Daphne said. 'Once he blows, he goes dormant for a while. And here's another secret: despite his abrasive manner, he will respect you if you stand up to him.'

'Like Zeke? He stands up to him. There's no love lost there.'

'Really? Why would you say that? Zeke is William's favorite.' She laughed. 'You just watch the way he looks at Zeke. Zeke's the only one of the bunch with a backbone. Just watch. You'll see what I mean.'

She said goodbye. I washed my hands and face, and had just entered the sitting room, when I heard someone crying. I moved over to the door of the dumbwaiter and opened it, just as Daphne had shown me. It was like turning on an intercom.

'... it's not like I had a choice.' The woman's voice had taken a hysterical turn. She was sobbing uncontrollably now.

'I cannot believe this.' Simon's shouting made matters worse. The woman started a fresh spate of sobs. 'This has gone on long enough. I've had it. I swear to you, Margaret, I've had about all I can handle.'

'Don't you dare act as though this is my fault.' The sobs were replaced by tearful shouting now. 'What am I supposed to do? With a baby? Me? I've very little money. The only thing I know how to do is run a stupid sewing machine. And do you think I'll get a reference or any help from your father? I won't. You know it.'

'I'll figure something out,' Simon said. 'Please, just trust me. I'll help you get through this. We'll get things handled, together.'

'I'll need to go away,' the woman said. 'I'll need enough money to live while I train for something. I don't mind hard work, I just need some help.'

'And I'll see that you get it, of that you can be sure.'

They must have moved to a different area in the study. Their words were mumbled now. Try as I might, I couldn't understand what they were saying, despite doing everything short of sticking my head down the dumbwaiter shaft. I stood up and caught a glimpse of myself in the mirror. My shoulders and hair were covered with dust. I changed my shirt, Simon's secret heavy in my heart.

… not like I had a choice. The girl's words kept running through my head. Had Simon forced himself on her?

Chapter 8

Daphne drove Granna and me to the Winslows' in an old Chevy sedan. She whipped along the country lanes at breakneck speed. Granna, who sat in the passenger seat, whooped with joy as we bumped along. I clung, white-knuckled, to the sides of my seat, expecting us to crash and roll any second.

'If the workers go on strike, the mill will all but shut down,' Daphne said. She jerked the wheel, just in time to dodge a pothole.

'Now that Zeke's here, Will Sr will have to give way. Those women deserve fair wages. Everyone knows the equipment needs updating. You just watch. Zeke will fix it,' Granna said. 'And if they don't fix—'

Her words were lost as we hit a rut and all four tires left the ground.

'Daphne, please,' I said.

She looked at me, a smile on her face.

'Better slow down on the Winslows' drive,' Granna shouted.

'I will,' Daphne said. 'Mother will be furious if I kick up dust.'

She slowed to normal speed as we turned into a wooded lane, which looped and curved around oaks with gnarled branches.

The house was very similar in size to the Caens', but where Zeke's family home was comfortable in an unpretentious way,

72

the Winslow house was immaculate. Even nature didn't dare defy Arliss Winslow. Not one shrub was amiss, not one leaf out of place. A white tent had been set up in front of the house with tables arranged around the circumference and a dance floor in the center. A trio played music while people milled around, sipping champagne from glasses kept full by the white-coated waiters. Behind the musicians, a myriad of other instruments rested in stands, all in readiness for the dancing that would take place after dinner. Torches would provide light after the sun went down.

I vowed if Zeke didn't show up by the time the dancing started, I would slip away from the party and take the footpath back to the Caen house for the quiet evening I coveted.

'I won't leave you alone if you don't want me to,' Granna said, as we headed up to the porch. She was dressed in a floor-length linen dress with a tall matching hat, forty years out of date. She wore the ensemble like a queen. Daphne walked before us, up the walkway to the front door which stood open.

'I need to go find my mother,' Daphne said. 'Granna, please behave yourself, if not for my sake, then for Sarah's.'

'She thinks I'm going to make a scene. Arliss and I do not get along very well.' Granna took a swig from her flask and offered it to me. I shook my head, unable to stomach whisky in the oppressive June heat. 'I can't face Arliss Winslow without whisky in my belly, and I'm not ashamed to admit it,' Granna said.

The Winslow house didn't have a proper foyer. The front door led into a big, open room, with high ceilings and a fireplace large enough to hold a side of beef with room to spare. The floor-to-ceiling bookcase which took up the entire wall held a smattering of books, their spines too pristine to have been read. Most of the shelf space was filled with Oriental vases and statues. The furniture had been removed from the room, with the exception of a few chairs. Tables set with chafing dishes were nestled in one corner. Uniformed maids moved around with purpose. In the background, Arliss Winslow hovered, barking out orders. People started to arrive in droves now, most of them stopping at the tent outside for the proffered champagne.

'Maybe we can go outside and avoid her altogether,' I said to Granna.

'That is not the way to deal with Arliss.' She grabbed my arm with a hawk-like grip and whirled me around.

'Shut that front door. I don't want the guests coming in here now. I want them in the pavilion until dinner is served.' Arliss's imperious voice rose above the hub.

She wore a long silvery dress. Her hair had been arranged on top of her head and held in place by an honest to god tiara. I wondered if she expected us to curtsey. I giggled. She looked down her long nose at me.

'Where's Zeke?'

'He's at the mill. He'll be here.'

'I'd have thought Zeke would want to be by your side when you make your entrance into Millport society.'

'Millport society?' Granna guffawed. 'Trying a little too hard, aren't you, Arliss?' Granna took a step closer to Arliss and gazed up at her without fear.

'You reek of whiskey,' Arliss said.

'What of it? I don't put on airs. I know from where I've come.'

'Enjoy yourselves,' Arliss said. And with a nod, she left us.

'I see she's still up to her old tricks.' A man with a thick shock of white hair stood next to Granna. Although he had a round belly, he stood tall and strong as he surveyed the room with shrewd and authoritative eyes.

'Ken,' she said, offering her cheek to him for the proffered kiss. 'Meet Zeke's wife, Sarah. Sarah, Ken Connor.'

'Oh,' I said, seeing the resemblance between Ken Connor, Wade and Joe. Although Ken's hair was white, he had the same intelligent eyes, but where Joe's eyes were serious, and Wade's expression full of intensity, Ken Connor smiled at me with kindness.

'Welcome to Millport,' he said. 'Lavinia and I wanted to see you and Zeke, perhaps have you over for a Sunday lunch. Are you enjoying it here?'

'I'm adjusting to the blistering heat,' I said.

Granna sipped from her flask and offered it to Ken. He took it and sipped as well.

'You always did have good taste in whisky.' He smiled as he handed the flask back to her. I stood by and listened while they spoke of the war, the speculation in the newspapers of Hitler's imminent assassination, gasoline rationing, and the impending strike at the mill. Soon Granna wandered off, leaving Mr Connor and me alone.

'She's a force to be reckoned with,' Ken said.

'She's been very kind,' I said. 'Do you mind if I ask you about Rachel Caen's case?' When a waiter walked by, Ken grabbed a glass of champagne. He took a sip and set the glass down on a nearby table. 'Of course not. Ask away.' He took a cigarette out of a silver case and stuck it in his mouth. He didn't light it. He just let it hang there for a moment. 'I can't really comment on an ongoing investigation. But I know who killed her, and I am in the process of getting proof. As god is my witness, I'll see that justice is served.'

'Why don't you tell Joe—'

'What are you two talking about so seriously?' Daphne stepped between us, all smiles and charm. 'How do you like Sarah, Ken? We've been having such fun. It's nice to have another woman at the house.'

'If you ladies will excuse me. Nice to meet you, Sarah.' Ken wove through the crowd and joined a group of men who were moving through the buffet line. Next to me, Daphne stood frozen, silent.

'What's wrong?' I asked.

She stared at Ken Connor's retreating figure as if she hadn't heard me. 'Daphne?'

'Nothing, other than Ken being a bit rude. He didn't even speak to me.' She smiled at me. 'Are you having a good time? My mother insists that I mingle, so I'm afraid I'm going to have to leave you on your own.'

'That's fine,' I said. 'I may get a plate of food and go find Granna.'

'Have you seen Simon? I thought he'd be here by now. Never mind. I'm sure he'll show eventually.'

Zeke stepped through the patio doors, spotted us, and smiled. 'Sorry to make you face this crowd alone.'

'I'm glad you're here, darling,' Daphne said. 'I need to do Mother's bidding, and I didn't want to leave Sarah without anyone to talk to. There she is now. Off I go.'

'I'm surprised Daphne is such an obedient daughter,' I said to Zeke.

'Arliss Winslow doesn't take no for an answer,' Zeke said. 'I'm sorry I'm late.'

'Crisis averted?'

'For now,' Zeke said. 'Father won't budge on the wage increase, but we've asked the workers for a two-day reprieve, and they agreed. I have a plan, but I can't do anything until I find Simon. Have you seen him?'

'No, but I met Ken Connor.' I made sure no one eavesdropped on our conversation. 'He says he knows who killed Rachel and that he's getting proof.'

Zeke shook his head. 'He's said that before, and nothing's ever come of it. Let's get out of here. Give me a few minutes and we'll slip out the back door.'

Zeke had his back to the party, so he didn't see Ken Connor break away from the buffet line and head toward us.

'Zeke? Can I talk to you for a minute?' Ken said.

'Sure,' Zeke said.

'Alone?' Ken looked at me.

'Of course,' I said. 'I'll just be outside, Zeke.'

'I won't be long,' Zeke said. He and Ken moved away from the throng and sat down in two chairs tucked into the corner of the room. I wandered around, aimless, not quite sure to whom I should speak.

'Penny for your thoughts?' A woman with kind eyes and gray hair peered at me. 'I'm Lavinia Connor. You must be Sarah?'

'Yes, I am,' I said.

'We're so glad that you and Zeke have come home,' she said. 'I saw you talking to my husband, and assumed you were speaking about Rachel. He gets a certain look on his face when he discusses her case. Not a day goes by that he doesn't go through his files, looking for some clue.' A tiny, bird-like woman, she looked up at me with brilliant blue eyes, her silver hair tufted atop her head like a nest. 'I think the past should be left alone, don't you?'

'I don't think that anyone should get away with murder,' I said.

'A woman of substance.' Lavinia smiled at me. 'How are you and Daphne getting along?'

'She's been very kind and welcoming,' I said. 'Do you live nearby?'

'No, dear. I live on the other side of town.' She leaned close to me. 'Have you heard about our cat burglar? It's quite exciting. The Van Elstens had their silverware taken while they were asleep in their beds.'

'Joe mentioned it to us when we arrived.'

'We don't get much excitement around here.' She sighed and met my eyes. 'You probably enjoy being out of the limelight.'

So she knew. I wondered how long it would take her to bring up the murder trial, and the newspapers headlines that didn't cast me in the light.

'I'm sorry. I didn't mean to embarrass you. I followed the trial, you know. I thought you were very brave,' she said. 'And I read about that woman who was going to kill her husband. You saved his life, too.'

'I wouldn't say I actually—'

77

'Nonsense. Take your credit, my dear! I, for one, am very proud to know you. Please promise that you will come to see us.'

'Lavinia.' I heard Arliss's hard, shrill voice before I saw her.

Lavinia and I stepped away from each other like two children caught raiding the cookie jar. 'There you are,' Arliss said. She ignored me completely. 'Would you please go and sit with Mrs Crowel? She has been guzzling the champagne. I want to make sure she doesn't embarrass herself.'

Arliss had elbowed her way between Lavinia Connor and me, all but cutting me out of the conversation.

'Of course,' Lavinia said. She gave me a pitying look before she walked toward the crowd under the tent, where a woman wearing a bright red wig and a green dress danced with two men. She held a champagne glass, its contents sloshing onto the floor and the people around her as she shook and shimmied. I would have laughed out loud if Arliss Winslow wasn't standing close, giving me the evil eye. The minute Lavinia Connor disappeared into the crowd, Arliss hissed, 'Don't be fooled by Lavinia Connor's kindness. You don't belong here. You will never be one of us. We don't want you.'

'I don't care,' I said. 'Moreover, I've become hardened to cheap gossip, so your words mean little.' I set my champagne glass down on the nearest table, gave Arliss a beaming smile, and walked away from her.

I meandered around, smiling at people, uttering trite responses to equally vapid questions, until I found Zeke, still engaged in conversation with Ken Connor. I caught his eye and pointed to the French doors that led outside. He nodded. I headed out to find a spot to wait for him, away from the crowd.

Several tables and chairs were nestled among boxed shrubs around the patio. The arrangement provided private seating areas for those wishing to take a break from the crowd. I found a little nook with a table for two, behind the large fountain. Just as I sat down, the music stopped, and the band took their first break.

The dancers moved to the buffet line. Arliss Winslow stepped up to the microphone on the bandstand, welcomed her guests, and invited them in to dinner. My encounter with Arliss had taken away my appetite, and I now welcomed the privacy.

I leaned back in my little chair, enjoying the night noises and the sound of the babbling fountain. Ken Connor's words kept running through my head. *'I know who killed her, and I am in the process of getting proof. As god is my witness, I'll see that justice is served.'*

My thoughts were interrupted when Sophie came out onto the terrace, looking like a schoolgirl playing dress-up in a black slinky gown, backless and clinging. She had on high heels and no stockings. One hand held a long, ebony cigarette holder, the other held a bottle of champagne. Sophie took a swig out of the bottle.

'Sophie, put that champagne down immediately before someone sees you.' Arliss Winslow charged at her daughter like a bull after a red cape.

Sophie moved out of her mother's way and took another swig of the bottle.

'Leave me alone, Mother. I'm not in the mood for you.'

'You're drunk.' Arliss made the pronouncement like a hanging judge.

'Indeed I am. And I plan to continue. So leave me alone.'

I eavesdropped without shame, enjoying Mrs Winslow's anger. Even though I didn't care for Sophie, I admired the way she stood up to her mother.

'I see you've run Sarah off,' Sophie said. 'Well done.'

'Keep your voice down. Get in the house now. Go upstairs and change your clothes. I'll send someone up with food and coffee. You can come down when you've sobered up. Either that, or you can stay in your room.'

'Knock it off, Mother. I'm tired of doing your bidding, tired of your senseless manipulations.' She took a puff of her cigarette and blew the smoke in Arliss's face. 'Frankly, Mother, I'm tired of you.'

The slap came out of nowhere. Hand on skin, loud and stinging. I peered at them through the box hedge. I held my breath, ready for Sophie, the brave rebel, to react. Her eyes flashed, and even in the dusk I could see the red outline of Arliss's hand starting to bloom on Sophie's white cheek.

'That'll knock some sense into you. Come in at once.' Arliss Winslow walked away from Sophie, confident that her daughter would follow. Sophie shrank before my eyes, defeated and beaten. I hated Arliss Winslow then. Sophie hung her head and followed her mother into the house, her proverbial tail tucked between her legs, when a figure stepped out of the shadows.

I covered my mouth to stifle the involuntary gasp. Joe took the champagne bottle from Sophie and set it down on a nearby table.

'What are you doing here?' I had to strain to hear Sophie's words.

'Trying to find a minute alone with you. It's not easy with your mother always trying to keep us apart.' I peered between the bushes as Joe moved close to Sophie and put his arm around her. Much to my surprise, she leaned into him. 'Why do you let her push you around like that?'

'Stop being so nice to me,' Sophie said. She pushed away from him and took a cigarette out of a small bag she carried. She tried to put it in the cigarette holder, but Joe wrested it away from her, tore it in half and threw it in one of the ashtrays that lay close by. 'Knock it off, Sophie. You know you hate smoking. What are you playing at? Why won't you marry me? Let me take care of you.'

Sophie reached up and touched Joe's cheek, a thousand words conveyed in that gentle caress.

'Sophie?' Arliss Winslow barked.

'Coming Mother,' Sophie called. 'I'm sorry, Joe.' She walked toward the house like a frightened child walking to the front of the class for a paddling.

I waited in the shadows as Joe slipped away. Time to find Zeke. I was leaving, with or without him.

We met on the patio.

'Let's get out of here,' he said. 'Do you mind walking?'

'Not if you don't.'

'My leg's not hurting,' he said. 'I'll get rid of this wretched cane one of these days.'

We headed toward the footpath that led through the woods to the Caen house. Moonlight flooded the path with silver light, showing us the way. When we got close to the abandoned barn, Zeke led me off the path.

'Come here. I want to show you something.' He took me into his arms and brushed my lips with his. We stood like that for a moment, enveloped by the soft strains of the music and the warm June breeze. 'Follow me.'

He took me to the abandoned barn. The old picnic table that sat in front of it was now covered with a linen tablecloth. Two empty wine bottles held candles, which Zeke lit. He reached under the table and surprised me with a bucket of champagne on ice and a wicker hamper from which he withdrew two China plates, two crystal champagne flutes, and a big serving platter wrapped in kitchen linens. Zeke unwrapped the linen to reveal a feast of cold chicken, deviled eggs, coleslaw, and potato salad.

'What is this?' I asked.

'An impromptu picnic at our old barn. We used to keep the horses here, until Daphne convinced my father to build her the new stables closer to the house. It's dry as tinder and really needs to be demolished. Simon, Will, and I used to play here when we were kids. Our sentiment has kept it standing.' He poured two flutes of champagne and handed one to me. 'That was the past. Now I am here with you. Thanks for coming home with me, Sarah. I know it hasn't been easy.' We held up our glasses in a silent toast.

81

'Mrs Griswold has done us proud,' Zeke said, as he piled food on a plate.

'This is perfect,' I said, realizing just how hungry I had become.

'It's nice to be alone with you,' Zeke said. 'Much better than Arliss Winslow's party.' The band started again, and 'Pennsylvania 6-5000' serenaded us. We listened, leaning against each other, enjoying the music, glad to be away from the crowd. The band played 'In the Mood,' 'A-Train,' the whole retinue of popular dance music.

'What were you and Ken Connor talking about?' Zeke tensed at my question. I persisted, nonetheless. 'Do the police think Simon had anything to do with Rachel's murder?'

'Finding the emeralds in his office didn't exactly endear him to the police. There's talk.'

'He didn't kill her,' I said. 'I'm sure of it.'

'How can you be so certain? You only just met him.'

I shrugged. 'Call it intuition, if you want. I just know in my heart that Simon didn't kill anyone. He's too …' I chose my words carefully, '… weak. I can see that he gambles and is a bit reckless when it comes to money, but your brother is not a murderer. And if he is arrested, I am going to clear his name.'

'If my brother's arrested, we will both clear his name. We'll work together. No secrets?'

'No secrets,' I said.

'Joe Connor won't be too happy to discover you meddling in one of his investigations.'

I took a sip of champagne. 'Joe Connor will have to deal with that.'

He kissed me. 'If you'll reach into the hamper, you'll find a tin with a large slab of chocolate cake in it.'

I reached under the table.

'There's another box as well, bring that out too.'

Zeke got two forks and we shared the cake, eating it right out of the tin. I reached for the leather box that Zeke had set on the table. 'What's this?'

82

'A little bird told me you took a fancy to it.'

There, nestled on the white silk which lined the box lay the fountain pen, the gold filigreed overlay gleaming in the moonlight.

'This is beautiful. You've got to stop spoiling me,' I said.

'Not a chance,' he said. 'I love the look on your face when I give you gifts.'

He kissed me, and I soon forgot about the pen, the chocolate cake, and everything else. 'You two are all over each other like children.' Simon walked into the clearing by the barn, dressed in work clothes, a serious look on his face.

'What are you doing here?' Zeke asked.

Simon took in our picnic, the champagne bottle turned upside down in the ice bucket. 'I'm sorry to interrupt your tete-a-tete, but we have a situation at the plant.'

'What? Simon, be serious. What could possibly require you to need me at the plant at ten-thirty at night?'

'A malfunction in one of the machines,' Simon said. 'Production has come to a full stop. Bob Napier thinks he can patch it together, but I don't think it will be safe. The men are coming in the morning to fix it, but we need to move things around so the repairmen can work. I was thinking the women could continue with sewing the fabric. At least we won't have to shut down completely—'

'Okay,' Zeke said. 'I'll take Sarah home and meet you there.'

'I've got my car at the road,' Simon said. 'I'll drive Sarah home and take you myself.' We didn't speak as we packed up our picnic. Simon helped us carry the baskets to the car, where we stowed them in the trunk. When we arrived at the house, Zeke walked me to the door, saw me safely in, and sped off with Simon.

Chapter 9

I awoke to a relentless pounding on the bedroom door. The bedside clock said seven-thirty.

'Go away,' Zeke called from the bedroom.

'It's me, Helen. Please, let me in.'

Zeke groaned.

'I'm coming,' I said. When I stood up, a throbbing pain started behind my eyes, the price I would pay for the champagne we had consumed last night.

I opened the door to Helen, whose eyes were swollen into slits from crying. She followed me into the room and sat down on the sofa.

'Sarah—' She could barely get the words out.

'Take a breath,' I said. I rubbed her back as I handed her a handkerchief. Zeke swept by me, on his way to the bathroom.

When Helen regained a semblance of control, I poured her a glass of water left over from yesterday. She gulped it.

'I'm so sorry for barging in on you, but when I heard the news—'

'What news?'

'There's been a murder.' She got the words out just as Zeke came out of the bathroom.

'What?' I said.

'Who?' Zeke said at the same time.

Helen's eyes welled with what promised to be a fresh spate of tears.

'Who?' Zeke asked again.

'Ken Connor,' Helen said. She buried her head in her hands and started to weep. Zeke closed the bedroom door behind him, while I tended to Helen. The only thing I could do was sit next to her, ready to offer comfort.

Zeke came out of the bedroom buttoning his shirt. 'I'm going to find out what's happened,' he said. Our eyes met. Neither one of us spoke. There was nothing to say.

I got a fresh handkerchief out of Zeke's drawer and handed it to Helen. While she blew her nose like a honking goose, I went into the bathroom and got her a cold washcloth.

'Thanks,' she said. She held the cloth over her face. Before too long her breathing stilled, as did she.

'I didn't realize you and Ken were so close,' I said.

'It's not that. It's just—'

Granna didn't bother to knock. She burst into the room and stopped short when she saw Helen sitting on my sofa.

'What's happened?'

'Ken Connor has been murdered,' I said.

She staggered over to the couch and sat down. The color drained from her face. She reached for her flask, held it to her lips, and changed her mind at the last minute.

'This is not good,' she said. 'Rachel – Ken – oh. This changes everything. You see that, don't you?' She looked at me, trying to convey some message. Her eyes lit on Helen's hunched-over form. 'Helen, I think it would be best if you went home for a few days. Would you like that?'

Helen nodded.

'Then run along and pack a bag. We'll see you home safely.' Granna's voice brimmed with authority.

'Yes, ma'am.' Helen was on her feet and out of the room in a flash.

'I didn't realize that she and Ken Connor were so close.'

'They're not close. Those weren't tears of sorrow. Helen is one of the most levelheaded young women I have ever met. Something's frightened her. That child is scared to death,' Granna said.

'Of what?'

Granna opened her mouth to speak but didn't have time to put her suspicions into words. Helen walked back into the room just then, her cloth valise in one hand, her felt hat in the other.

* * *

Helen didn't speak as we walked to the cottage she shared with her father in town. The shingled cottage was neat as a pin, with a rose garden in the front yard. Around the back, I caught a glimpse of a raised vegetable garden and a white sheet flapping on a clothes line, like a symbol of surrender. We stopped on the path which led up to the porch. A man stood in the shadow of the porch, watching us. I gave Helen some money, with the promise of more if she needed it.

'I hope you come back, Helen,' I said.

'I don't think so, miss,' she said. And with a dejected air, she headed up the stairs.

The man who waited for Helen wouldn't meet my eyes as he took his daughter's bag and followed her into the house. I headed back to the place I – at least for the moment – called home.

* * *

Three police cars were parked in the front yard when I approached the house. One policeman stood outside the open front door, while another stood just outside the patrol car, talking into the radio. Two uniformed officers came outside. Simon walked between them, his hands cuffed in front of him. Joe Connor followed behind, a grim look on his face. The officers put Simon in the back seat and drove off just as I reached them, leaving me standing in a cloud of dust.

I ran up the porch steps and into the hallway, following the voices that were in the study. Part of me wanted to run upstairs and lock my bedroom door behind me, but I knew my duty. Zeke would want me with him. I knocked twice on the study door and opened it. Granna, Daphne, Will Sr, and Zeke were in the room. They had stopped speaking, the still hush between them creating a vacuum. Will Sr sat behind his desk, his face florid and covered in sweat. Zeke paced back and forth before the window, his limp pronounced, his cane clutched in his hand with a white-knuckled grip. Daphne sat on the sofa, dressed in breeches and her tall leather boots, staring into space, while Granna sat with her hands folded in her lap, her eyes closed.

'What's happened?'

'Simon's been arrested for Rachel's murder,' Zeke said.

Chapter 10

Zeke moved over to the fireplace. He stood before it now, leaning on his cane. He held out his hand, beckoning me to take my place beside him.

'I cannot believe that Simon would disgrace me and this family with his aberrant behavior. This is intolerable. He will be removed from the firm and cut off without a penny. I shall call Mitchell Springer—'

'You'll do no such thing,' Zeke said.

'Don't smart mouth me, young man. Simon can rot in jail for all I care, and I don't need you or that meddling wife of yours telling me what to do.'

'Shut up, William,' Granna snapped.

The room fell silent.

'You'll let Zeke deal with this. He's the only levelheaded one in this family, and you know it.'

Will Sr glared at her for a moment. We braced ourselves for battle, but nothing happened.

'Zeke, what do you propose to do?' Granna asked.

'Sarah and I will go down to the station and get Simon out of jail. That's the first step. While we're there, we'll find out what evidence they have. They must have come across something, or they wouldn't have come and arrested him.'

'Isn't that obvious?' Daphne sniffed into a pristine white handkerchief. 'They found one of Rachel's emeralds in his room. What can he say to that?'

'We all know that Simon has not murdered anyone. Someone planted those emeralds. I plan to find out who and why,' Zeke said.

'I'll arrange a criminal lawyer,' Daphne said.

'You will not.' William Sr almost shouted the words.

'Good idea,' Zeke said, ignoring his father. 'Mitchell Springer has no experience in this area. Daphne, you see to that. Sarah and I will see what we need to do to arrange bail. When we get home, Father, we are going to talk about the future.'

'You do not dictate the agenda around here,' William Sr said.

'Come with me?' Zeke asked, holding out his hand for me.

He didn't have to ask twice.

* * *

As we were leaving, Toby came down the stairs, tears running down his cheeks. 'Where's Papa? I want Papa.' Daphne picked him up, making reassuring sounds as she carried him back upstairs.

Zeke screeched out of the driveway and onto the dirt road. Soon we left the shade of the trees and were whizzing along toward town, toward the jail, toward Simon and his mess.

'What are you thinking about?' Zeke asked. He didn't take his eyes off the road.

'I need to tell you about something I overheard. It's about Simon, and you're not going to like it.'

'Surely things cannot get any worse,' Zeke said.

'He was talking to a woman named Margaret. Simon was shouting, so it was hard not to listen. She's pregnant. I think Simon is the father.'

'What did you hear?'

'She said she needed money to live on, and a reference. She's going away – she worked at the mill, I think. He promised to help her.'

I didn't tell Zeke about the desperation in her voice, or how I came to eavesdrop by listening down the dumbwaiter shaft. Zeke was silent for a few moments.

'We need to stay here until I get things settled with the business and with my little brother.'

'I know,' I said.

'I want to oust father from the company,' Zeke said. 'If Granna and Simon vote with me, we can take away his power. Do you mind staying here for a few months? Once Simon's name is cleared, I'll need to stay on and see that he's able to handle the business. This, of course, is contingent upon the others agreeing to it.'

'Of course,' I said.

We parked and headed toward the stationhouse. Just as we walked into the police station, Zeke grabbed my hand. 'I'm sorry that you have to deal with this, with my family,' he said.

I thought of the ordeal my father put him through last October at Bennett House. Zeke had ostensibly come to work as my father's secretary. We discovered that he was working undercover. He hadn't been honest with us. But then my father hadn't been honest with him. I gave him a sheepish smile. 'We're even now,' I said.

'Yes, my love, I believe we are.' He smiled and held the door for me. The clacking of typewriter keys, the voices, the sound of footsteps as officers and clerical workers busied about ceased when Zeke and I entered the building. Every single person stopped what they were doing and stared at us as we walked toward the central desk to find out about Simon.

'They think Simon killed Ken Connor, too, don't they?'

'Seems like it. And Ken Connor was one of their own, so they'll be out for vengeance.'

'We'll prove he didn't do it. We'll prove he is innocent,' I said.

'We will certainly try.' Zeke turned to the desk sergeant. 'I'm here for my brother.'

The man behind the desk raised his eyes from the newspaper spread out before him. 'Simon Caen?'

Zeke leaned closer to the man, his voice low when he spoke. 'He's innocent until proven guilty. Take me to him. Now.'

'Zeke, Sarah,' Joe Connor called out from his open office door. 'Let them back, sergeant. I'll take them to Simon.' We went into Joe's office. He closed the door behind us and closed the blinds for privacy. Another man sat at Joe's desk. He was short and wide, with a thatch of mousy-colored frizz atop his head. His eyes were frog-like behind thick glasses. I disliked him on sight.

'Donald Bateson,' Zeke said.

'That's Detective Bateson,' the man said.

'Naturally, I can't work Father's case,' Joe said. 'I'll stay on the jewelry thefts, and Donald will work the murder.'

'Unless we discover they are connected,' Detective Bateson said.

'You think Ken's murder and the jewel heists are connected?' Zeke asked Detective Bateson.

'We found four more emeralds with the stolen items recovered at your home. They were in the bottom of the bag, so we missed them at first glance. Since we are operating on the assumption that whoever has the emeralds was involved in Rachel Caen's and Ken Connor's murder, it stands to reason that since the emeralds were found with the stolen items, the matters are related. Everyone knew that Ken was obsessed with Rachel's case. He must have come across something.'

'What a perfect set-up,' I said.

'Did you even ask him for an alibi?' Zeke asked.

'He wouldn't tell me where he was last night. I know Mrs Winslow had a party, but Simon wasn't there.'

'I think the cat burglar and the murders are separate. Maybe the same person murdered Ken Connor and Rachel, but the cat burglar is a thrill-seeker,' I said.

91

'My sentiments exactly,' Joe said.

'And …' I wanted to say Simon had been set up, but by whom? Someone in Zeke's house?

'Mrs Caen,' Detective Bateson took a white handkerchief out of his pocket and polished his glasses. 'I am sure that you are an intelligent woman, but you have no expertise in these matters. Don't you think it's best to stay home, have some children, cook some meals, and take care of your husband?' He put his glasses back in his pocket, stood up, and headed for the door. 'Zeke, I'll be coming around to your house to take statements from your family. And I'll want to speak to Simon again, so see that he doesn't go anywhere.'

'Go easy on my mother,' Joe said.

'Of course,' Detective Bateson said. 'Give me fifteen minutes, and you can take her home.'

He didn't say goodbye. He just walked out the door, leaving us in a vacuum after he shut it behind him. The three of us stood for a moment, unsure what to say to each other. Zeke broke the silence.

'Donald Bateson, a detective?' Zeke asked Joe. 'How did that happen?'

'We needed someone and most of the men are off fighting,' Joe said.

'That does not bode well for Simon,' Zeke said. 'Those two have hated each other since they were old enough to fight in the sandbox.'

'He is a bit full of himself,' Joe said.

'You realize that I am going to work on this myself,' Zeke said. 'I won't step on his toes, but that man is out to prove Simon murdered your father. I am going to be working just as hard to prove he didn't.'

'I trust you to be discreet,' Joe said. 'I agree with you, Sarah. I don't think the thefts and the murders are connected. But I have a feeling that the emeralds are tied to Rachel's murder and

92

my father's murder. It's the only thing that makes sense, especially given my father's singular obsession with proving that Rachel didn't kill herself.'

You have no idea, I thought.

'Simon didn't do it,' Zeke said. 'I'm sure of it.'

'I agree,' Joe said. 'Let's take you to him. After which I am going to loiter in front of Detective Bateson's office. I will not have that idiot haranguing my mother.'

* * *

The jailhouse was on the second floor of the police station. Four jail cells opened into the lobby, each cell equipped with a small cot, complete with a gray blanket and a pillow. All the cells were empty. A sole metal desk and two chairs for visitors were the only pieces of furniture in the room. An officer sat there now, reading the newspaper. Another uniformed officer stood outside a closed door.

'I have him in the interview room,' Joe said. He nodded at the officer who guarded the door.

Simon sat at the table, his head buried in his hands. He glared at us with red, swollen eyes as we walked into the room.

'Where's Daphne?'

'Home with your son,' Zeke said.

'This is so ridiculous,' Simon said.

'Stop. Just stop. I'm doing the talking now, Simon. Mind how you speak to me, or I will take my wife, leave Millport, and you can sort this mess out yourself.'

'I didn't kill her,' Simon said, his voice full of anger and indignation.

'I know it. And I'm going to prove it, but you need to lose your arrogant attitude and realize that you are in serious trouble.'

Simon looked at me, his eyes imploring and desperate. I saw fear there, and for the first time, I realized the gravity of Simon's situation.

'Where were you last night after we met at the mill?' Zeke asked.

Simon took a deep breath.

'Don't even think about lying to me. Were you gambling?' Zeke set his cane on the table and moved to the corner of the room. He leaned against the wall, his arms folded over his chest. 'Where did you get the money to pay off your gambling debts?'

Simon said nothing. He just sat at the table, his head cradled in his hands.

'You'd better tell me about Margaret,' Zeke said.

Simon raised his head and looked at Zeke with his swollen, bloodshot eyes. 'What do you know of Margaret?'

'I know that she's pregnant, and that you at least had the decency to help her,' Zeke said. 'Really, Simon. You're lucky Daphne doesn't divorce you—'

'Divorce me? Wait a second. You think that I—' He laughed, a grating sound filled with hysteria. 'You think I got that poor girl pregnant? You think I would stoop that low?'

'Just tell me what happened, Simon. Please. Just tell me.'

'Not in front of her,' Simon said.

'She stays. She's my wife. She's part of this family.'

'It's Father,' Simon said. 'He led that poor young woman on and made her think that he was in love with her. He told her he wanted to marry her.'

'Surely you don't believe for a minute that our father would …' Something changed in Zeke's expression. He experienced a revelation, the strength of which morphed his entire being from that of surprise to anger. 'My god, he did it, didn't he?'

'He did. It's not the first time either.' Simon warmed to his subject. He stood and started to pace. 'As far as I know he hasn't gotten any of them pregnant before, but I noticed he had an eye for the young female workers my first day on the job. And as for Margaret, she is a smart girl, a good worker. I overheard Father talking to her one day, promising her the moon.

'When she found out she was pregnant, she needed help. She didn't want to make any trouble. When she went to speak to Father, he wouldn't even let her in his office. She came to me for help. I had to do something. Her own family has all but disowned her. I gave her enough money to get by for a year, bought her a simple gold wedding ring and a man's gold band, to lend authenticity to her story of a dead husband. Last night, I drove her to Chesterton and put her on the train for Los Angeles.'

Zeke sighed. 'Okay, I believe you. I need to know where you got the money to pay your gambling debts.'

'From Daphne,' Simon said.

'Where did she get the money?' Zeke asked.

'I have no idea. You'll have to ask her.'

* * *

Zeke paid Simon's bail. Fifteen minutes later we were driving home. Simon sat sullen in the backseat, not speaking to either one of us. When we drove through town, Zeke turned off Main Street and drove through a residential neighborhood. All the houses were two stories, most were painted white. Trees with gnarled limbs graced front lawns that were perfectly maintained. Zeke parked in the shade in front of one of the houses.

'What are you doing?' Simon asked.

'I need to talk to you.' Zeke switched off the engine and turned around to face his brother. 'I've had it with Father. He exploits everything he touches. I'm going to talk to Granna when we get home. You, Granna, and I form a quorum. I want to vote father out of the company. We have enough troubles with the workers. His actions with Margaret are not going to help things.'

'You're playing with fire,' Simon said.

'I don't care. I want him gone. We'll make the changes that you want. As soon as the company is running smoothly, Sarah

95

and I will leave. The question is, will you commit to managing things after I'm gone?'

'It's time I grew up and took some responsibility.' He wiped his eyes. 'If you make a motion, I'll vote in your favor.'

* * *

Daphne, Toby, and Granna waited for us outside. Daphne, dressed in her riding breeches and her boots, her face twisted into a scowl, was not pleased to see her husband. Granna stood near her, Toby clinging to her leg. When the car pulled up to the house, Toby broke away from Granna and tore down the steps. Simon jumped out of the car and scooped Toby into his arms, holding the child close to his heart.

'Daddy, where did you go? You're not leaving us, are you?'

'Of course I'm not,' Simon said.

'Granna, Sarah and I need to talk to you. Where's Father?'

'In his study,' Granna said.

Toby, Simon, and Daphne had walked into the house together. Zeke told Granna of his plan to oust his father from the company. Granna agreed and promised to support Zeke. Zeke grabbed my hand as we headed up the stairs, toward the eye of the storm.

'Let me speak to Daphne, alone, would you? Go in with Granna, and I'll be with you in a minute.'

'Of course,' I said.

Zeke went off to find Daphne. I followed Granna into the study where Will Sr sat behind his desk. A crystal glass sat on a coaster near his elbow, half-full of the Scotch that he preferred, even though it was only eleven-thirty. He hid behind the newspaper and pretended to read.

'Hitting it a little early, aren't you?' Granna asked.

'Like you haven't been known to sip from that flask you have in your pocket,' Will Sr said. He ignored us and continued to read the paper.

We sat down on the sofa under the window.

'What're you doing in here? Don't you have someplace else to be?'

'Zeke wants to talk to us,' Granna said, 'about the mill.'

'What about the mill?'

'I really don't know, Will. We're just going to have to wait and see what Zeke says.'

He went back to his paper until Zeke and Simon came in. Simon carried a folder under his arm. He withdrew a document from it and placed it on the desk in front of Will Sr.

'What's the meaning of this?' Will Sr asked.

'Turn to page seven,' Simon said.

'Why?'

'We are having a meeting of the board of directors, as provided in Article 17, subsection (c).'

Will Sr picked up the document. He skimmed it and tossed it aside with a grunt.

'We're voting you out, Father,' Zeke said.

Simon stepped away from the desk.

'I will not stand for this rubbish.' Will Sr slammed his hand down on his desk. Simon jumped. Granna didn't flinch. Zeke moved closer to his father.

'Don't,' he said, in that calm voice. 'We know about Margaret. You know she's pregnant? She came to you for help and you ignored her. You should be ashamed of yourself. Simon had the decency to help her. He gave her enough money to have the child and get herself situated.'

'He'd better not have used corporate funds,' Will Sr said.

'I did.' Simon found his voice after all. 'I gave her one thousand dollars. I'd have given her more, so you'd best consider yourself lucky.'

Will Sr blustered for a minute, until he reached for the folder that Simon handed him and read it again, more slowly this time.

'I make a motion to oust William Caen Sr from the Millport Fabric Works Corporation,' Zeke said.

97

Simon seconded.

'All in favor?'

'I'm in favor,' Granna said. She stared at her son with a look of disgust.

'You are to stay away from the mill and all of the girls that work there. Do you understand?' She spat the words at him.

Will Sr pushed away from the desk, and without a backward glance, walked out of the room.

Seconds after the door slammed, Daphne stormed into the room, her cheeks flushed, her eyes ablaze.

'You want to know where I got the money to pay off Simon's debts?' She carried a small burlap sack with a drawstring. She came to a stop before the desk, undid the string, and dumped a wad of bills onto the desk. 'That's where.'

'Daphne, where did you get that?' Simon asked.

'Oh, shut up, Simon. I am so tired of you. There's twenty-seven-hundred dollars there.'

'Daphne, where did you get this money?' Simon asked, as he moved toward the desk.

When he reached a hand out, as if to touch it, Daphne slapped his hand away.

'Keep your hands off of it. That is for Toby,' she said. She leaned against the desk, positioning herself between Simon and the wad of bills. 'My husband has a gambling problem. Most of the time he loses, but sometimes he wins. He always comes home drunk. I check his pockets and keep what I find there. It's a habit now. He never knows how much he's got. I have got to look out for my son. God knows, his father won't. I hope you trust him with the mill, Zeke. I certainly wouldn't.' She gathered the money, stuffing it back into the sack, and left us.

'I had no idea,' Simon said.

Neither Zeke, Granna, nor I spoke. Zeke and Simon both looked shocked. Granna, on the other hand, had the faint beginning of a smile etched into her mouth.

'Something's not right,' Simon said. 'I would remember if I had won that much money.'

'Just leave it, Simon, will you?' Zeke said.

'I'll just go find Toby then,' Simon said. He gave Granna and me a wan smile, and headed off to find his child.

'I need to get out of here,' Zeke said. 'Do you mind if I go for a walk by myself?'

'No,' I said.

'See you soon.' He kissed my cheek and left Granna and me alone in the office.

'How are you coping, Granna?'

'I'm fine,' she said. 'I will always be fine. It's about time Simon grew up.'

Chapter 11

Will Sr disappeared. No one knew where he went after his family voted him out of the business. A search by Mrs Griswold revealed he had packed a bag and taken the majority of his clothes, without bothering to say goodbye to anyone. He left no forwarding address, so we had no way to contact him. The mood lifted in his absence, and before long the household slipped into a quiet routine.

Zeke and Simon made plans for the mill. They informed the workers that the mill would close for a two-week equipment upgrade. The women were happy when Simon told them not only would they be paid for the two weeks the mill was closed, they would receive an immediate bonus and a fair raise when they returned to work. Millport Fabric Works was to be one of the few places that paid its female workers the same wages as the men. There were a million details to be tended to, and Zeke needed to do the tending.

Zeke's frantic schedule posed little difficulty for me. Dr Geisler's handwritten notes flooded in daily, in a fat envelope addressed to me in his familiar scrawl. This suited me fine, as it gave me an excuse to stay sequestered in my room as I transcribed his written notes on my typewriting machine.

While all these things were happening at home and at the mill, an undercurrent of worry for Helen ran through my subconscious. She knew something. I half expected Rachel's ghost to appear and tell me what to do next, but alas, she was noticeably absent. Granna had all but told me to leave the girl alone, but I couldn't let it go. Helen knew something. I needed to know what that something was.

The mill had been closed three days when I decided to go to her.

I planned to slip out of the house unnoticed but was waylaid by a group of reporters who were staked out where the drive met the roadway.

The reporters had come after Ken Connor's death. Just a few at first, but it didn't take long for one of the more tenacious of them to figure out Ken's role as the lead investigator of Rachel's murder. His murder, along with the discovery of the emeralds in Portland – now common knowledge, and in all the papers – had brought the media to Millport, and to the Caen house, in force. I ducked behind the trunk of a very large tree, lucky to have done so before they saw me.

I counted ten of them, all drinking coffee and smoking cigarettes. They laughed and talked and threw their empty cups on the grass. Every single one of them smoked one cigarette after another. They left their ground cigarette butts on the street. They waited, like vultures stalking a carcass. Some had cameras on straps held around their necks, ready to memorialize our pain in a picture. One man stood out from the crowd. I recognized him right away. His hair was longer than the others. He didn't wear a hat, suit or tie. He dressed like a dock worker. Nick Newland, the newspaper reporter who hounded me since Jack Bennett's trial and the painful time after, when I took refuge at the Geisler Institute, grateful for a job. Nick's presence in Millport did not bode well for our desire to stay out of sight.

'Sarah, come here. They'll see you.' Granna hissed at me from behind a row of hedgerows, away from prying eyes. 'Where are you going?'

'I'm going to find Helen. Please don't talk me out of it. I'm so worried about her.' I wanted to go alone but knew that Granna would insist on coming with me.

She squinted at me. 'You're a stubborn one, aren't you? Very well. Come with me,' she said. 'Daphne and I will get you there.' I had no choice but to follow her back to the house.

Fifteen minutes later, Daphne, Granna, and I stood in the foyer, plotting a means of escape.

'I don't think we need to go to so much trouble,' I said.

'We do, my dear,' Granna said. 'The majority of our business is for the government, for the war effort. We don't want a lot of people around our family right now.'

'You're making parachutes,' I said.

'We're making products for the war, and we are vulnerable to sabotage. Any manufacturer is,' Daphne said. 'We don't need the publicity. Now come on. Let's go find Helen.'

'I think we should take her down the back trail. We can walk,' Granna said.

'Nope. There are reporters camped out near the intersection where the dirt and paved roads meet. We need to take the car.'

'And how are we going to do that?' Granna asked.

'We are going to walk to the stable – they can't see us do that from the road – and take my car. I parked it there this morning and walked home after my riding lesson. We can have Sarah duck in the back seat and fly past them.'

'Good thinking.' Granna said.

The sun beat down upon us as we slipped out the back door and walked through the vegetable garden toward the stable. Gleaming white clouds, full of the rain we so desperately needed, hung heavy in the sky. Birds chirped in the bushes, and squirrels rustled in the trees over our heads. The horses grazed in the pasture, ignoring us as we climbed over the fence and walked past them. There wasn't a soul around when we climbed into Daphne's car. I got in the back, clutching a stable blanket. I got down on the floorboards and Daphne and Granna tossed the blanket over me.

True to her word, Daphne hit the accelerator as the reporters swarmed the car.

'Stay down, Sarah,' she said.

I said a prayer as I did so.

'Daphne, he's blocking the road,' Granna said.

The engine roared.

'You're going to hit him,' Granna shouted.

I closed my eyes and waited for the crash. After about twenty seconds the car slowed, and Granna breathed.

'You can sit up, Sarah,' Daphne said.

'What happened?'

'You scared me, Daphne,' Granna said. 'You nearly ran over that young man.'

She smiled at Granna. 'But I didn't, did I? He got out of my way, and we're free of them.' Ten minutes later we pulled up in front of Helen's house.

'I'd like to speak to her alone, please,' I said. They didn't protest. Daphne let me out. Once I was up to the door, she drove away, in search of a shady place to park her car and wait for me.

The cottage had a desolate feel today. Someone had picked the roses from the bushes in the front yard. New buds were coming on, and in a few weeks, new flowers would bloom. I stepped onto the sun porch and went through to the main door of the cottage. I rapped on it. Nothing. I rapped again and strained to hear the footsteps in the house. Soon the front door opened and a short, solid-looking man came out the front door.

'Hello.' I peered through the screen. 'I'm Sarah Caen. I've come about Helen.'

'I know who you are, and I know why you've come.' His voice

was gruff at first, but after a moment, his manners took over, and he opened the screen door for me.

'I'll speak to you out here.' He stepped onto the sunporch, shutting the door behind him. He held out his hand, and I shook it. It was a strong hand, dry and calloused from labor. Two wooden chairs were arranged on the porch so they looked out on the street. Mr Dickenson sat in one and beckoned me to sit in the other.

'I'm sorry to come unannounced,' I said, 'but I really must see Helen. She left in such a hurry.'

'She's not here,' the man said. 'She's left. Scared to death, she was. And I'll not go and give her away. Not even to you, who she trusts.'

'I am worried for her safety.'

'She said that you'd be around, that you'd want to help her. But there's nothing you can do, not you or that husband of yours. Helen's afraid. Said the only sensible thing for her to do is go away. She's got a good head on her shoulders, does my Helen. If she says she needs to go away, then I say let her go.'

'Mr Dicks—'

'Nothing you can say will change my mind, ma'am. She made me promise. Our household takes a promise seriously.'

I took an envelope out of my pocketbook and handed it to Mr Dicks.

'Here's her wages. If she needs anything – money, help, whatever – will you contact me?'

'I'll see that she gets the money, ma'am, as she'll be needing it. As for the other, I'll not be making any promises that I can't keep.' He stood, my polite cue to vacate the premises. I followed suit, thanked Mr Dickenson for his time, and headed toward the street. Daphne and Granna had parked the car in the shade down the street. Just before I got in, I glanced back at the house. Mr Dickenson had gone inside and shut the door behind him.

'Well, where is she?' Daphne asked.

'He wouldn't tell me. Helen made him promise.'

'Why is she being so secretive?' Daphne asked.

'Because the girl saw something,' Granna said. 'She knows who put those emeralds and the stolen goods in Simon's desk.'

'Don't be ridiculous, Granna. How in the world would Helen know that? She has no reason to be in that part of the house.'

'Daphne, sometimes I wonder at you. That girl's been cleaning Simon's room and ironing his shirts for months now. Mrs Griswold doesn't know it. Simon's been paying her extra for it. It's a good thing, as far as I can see. The girl wants to go to school and be a teacher.' Granna blew her nose. 'I'm betting she was in the room when whoever it was dropped off the bag of loot. Helen saw something. Must have. Something's got her scared.'

'Is this true?' Daphne asked me.

'I'm afraid so,' I said. 'Helen wouldn't tell us what frightened her, but she was afraid. Of that I am certain.'

Daphne took a different route home and succeeded in avoiding the reporters. We parked the car in the garage and were just about to head to the house, when Daphne addressed Granna and me.

'If Helen's in danger, maybe we should leave her alone. Whatever's going on here, she's out of it. Maybe she should stay that way.'

'You're right.' I knew as I spoke the words that I would never leave Helen to fend for herself, not in a million years.

* * *

I went downstairs for a fresh pitcher of ice water and found the entire family, including Sophie, gathered in the study. Sophie didn't speak to me. In fact, she acted as though I weren't in the room at all. Simon sat in one of the chairs, an empty glass in his hand. Zeke sat in the chair next to him, his feet propped up on the ottoman. When he saw me, he gave me a tired smile.

'What news of Helen?' Simon asked.

'She's fled,' Daphne said. 'Didn't even tell her father where she went. Looks like you'll have to clean your messes up by yourself.'

'Daphne—'

'Don't *Daphne* me.' She moved over to the window, as if to get as far away from Simon as possible.

'You don't think Will Sr tried to … you know, like he did to Margaret,' Sophie said.

'How did you know about that?' Daphne asked.

'Don't look so surprised. Everyone knew. Margaret Petty isn't the first woman Will Sr seduced. He's a handsome man with a lot of money. He's old, but he's got a certain charm. Not for me. I never really liked him – sorry.' She looked at Zeke and Simon. 'Any number of young women in town – especially the new girls who work in the mill – would love a chance to marry a man with that much wealth and influence.'

'What?' Zeke couldn't keep the disgust from his voice.

'You haven't been here in a while, so, of course, you wouldn't know. Will Sr was quite the rogue. He flirted with all the girls at the mill. As far as he was concerned, they were all fair game. The locals knew what he was about, so they didn't pay him any mind. Daph, you knew that, right?' She looked at the entire group. 'I thought everyone knew that. I've often wondered if he didn't try to, you know, with Rachel. She was so beautiful.'

'Shut your mouth, Sophie,' Daphne said.

Did Will Sr murder Rachel? I glanced at Zeke. Our eyes met.

'Is there anything else about my father, or anyone else for that matter, that I need to know?' Zeke said.

'If Helen saw someone put those emeralds in my room, she'll come forward,' Simon said. 'I have every faith in that girl. She's got backbone.'

'Really, Simon,' Daphne said. 'Don't you think you're putting a little too much stock in a servant? Why in the world would she

106

save you? God knows, I wouldn't if I were in her shoes.' With that, Daphne strode from the room, slamming the door behind her.

* * *

Without Helen to oversee things, I had forgotten to shut the curtains in our room. I turned on the fan, took off my stockings, and stripped down to my slip. Working in my undergarments, I managed to transcribe five pages of handwritten notes before Daphne interrupted.

'Sarah,' Daphne called out. 'Detective Bateson wants to see you now. Can you open up, please?'

'Just a minute.' I threw my clothes on and opened the door to Daphne. She barged in without waiting for my invitation. 'A Nick Newland called for you. He said you were a friend and he wanted to make sure you were okay. I told him that I may be from the country, but I knew a city reporter when I heard one, and that he was not to call here again. I hope that was okay?'

'Perfect,' I said. 'Thank you.'

'They're waiting for you downstairs.'

'Daphne, if I wanted to walk into town and avoid the reporters, do I just take the same bridle trail we used earlier?'

'Yes. Do you want me to go with you?'

'No, that's okay. I need to walk and be alone, if you don't mind.'

'I understand. They're waiting for you in the study.' She left me, shutting the door behind her.

I splashed cold water on my face and headed downstairs. Detective Bateson sat at Will Sr's desk. A uniformed police officer sat in the corner behind him, a steno pad at the ready.

'Mrs Caen, please take a seat.' His voice was sweet as syrup. 'I understand you found the bag of stolen items in the desk in Mr Caen's room.' He took a document out of the folder that rested on the top of the desk and read it, taking his sweet time. *Two can play this game.* I leaned back and crossed my legs, as though I hadn't a care in the world.

'Would you mind telling me what you were doing in Simon's room? Do you normally go snooping through other people's things? I know women are curious creatures, but really.' The detective smiled at the policeman in the corner, as if to say, 'Isn't she ridiculous?'

'I got lost,' I said. 'I needed to go up to my room, the door was open, so I went in. The curtain moved, and I thought someone was there, so I walked to the window. That's when I noticed the canvas bag sticking out of the drawer.'

'Detective, I'm worried about Helen Dicks. She's missing. She may have seen whoever put the emeralds in Simon's room. I'm afraid she's in danger.'

Detective Bateson read his report, not bothering to acknowledge my words.

'Are you going to look for her?'

He looked up at me, a condescending smile on his face.

'Don't you worry, Mrs Caen,' he said. 'We'll take care of everything. I don't think I have any other questions. You are free to go.'

'You're not the least bit interested in Helen, are you?' I stood up.

'Mrs Caen, I'm going to give you some advice. Please don't take this the wrong way, but I have a lot of experience in matters such as this.' He gave me that smile again. 'Women just shouldn't think too much. It disturbs the constitution. Now run along. If we need anything, we'll let you know.'

I almost slammed the door but caught myself just in time. I would not let Detective Bateson see just how angry he made me.

* * *

I don't know what propelled me to the nursery, but I found myself standing in the doorway watching Simon and Toby. Simon sat at the child-sized table that Toby used for arts and crafts, a pencil in his hand, as he rendered an expert sketch of a horse's head.

'It's all about the ears,' Simon said. 'Once you master the place-ment of the ears, you've got it down pat.'

Toby stood next to his father, rapt, his eyes transfixed on his father's hand as it flew across the paper. He reached out and placed his little hand on his father's arm. Simon stopped drawing, set the pencil down, and wrapped his arms around the child, hugging him tight.

'You're a good boy, Toby,' Simon said.

'I know,' Toby said. 'That's why you should buy me a pony.'

I laughed. When Toby saw me, he ran toward me, throwing his arms around my waist.

'Aunt Sarah, come and see.' He took me by the hand and led me to the table.

'I need to talk to you.' I looked at Simon and pointed toward the door that led to the hallway.

'Toby, why don't you try to color over my pencil markings? Just trace along the top of them.'

It didn't take long for Toby to get lost in his coloring. Simon followed me out into the hallway. When we faced each other, I noticed that his face was gaunt and drawn, and that his pants hung off his frame.

'What's wrong?' Simon asked.

'Simon, do you realize if Helen saw whoever put the stolen goods and the emeralds in your room she could be in danger? She's fled, and no one knows where she is.'

Simon stared at me, his mind processing my words.

'I'm scared to death for her. How can I find her? She might be able to clear your name. In any event, she needs protection.'

'Have you spoken to the police?'

I snorted. 'Detective Bateson has no regard for anything I

might say. Who would she turn to in times of trouble? Tell me, Simon.'

'The man is a fool. Try the postmistress. She and Helen are thick as thieves. And don't worry about Detective Bateson. I'll deal with him.' Simon ran his hand over his face. 'I'm going to help you. We are going to find Helen and bring her here. I'll see to her safety myself.'

Spoken like a lover, I thought.

'Thank you,' I said.

* * *

Back in my room, I changed into my most comfortable shoes and set out the back door for the bridle path – the safest way to avoid the reporters – for my second long walk of the day. It was getting on five o'clock. The shadows grew long. The trees along the path provided enough shade to make the trek in the heat bearable. Once I reached the town, I knew I would have to be careful. Nick Newland would be like a bulldog on my scent, tracking me without mercy. When I reached Main Street, I ducked into an alley and studied my surroundings. My diligence paid off, for Nick Newland and Arliss Winslow stood together before the stationer's, their heads bent together, Nick listening while Arliss gave him an earful. I shook off my worry. There was nothing to be done about Arliss Winslow or Nick Newland. They walked toward the café. Once they had slipped inside, I crossed the street and hurried into the post office.

A woman with pale skin, jet black hair, and blood-red lips sat behind the counter. She sorted envelopes into various piles in front of her, humming while she worked.

'May I help you?'

'I'm not sure. I'm a friend of Helen Dicks,' I said.

'Aren't you Zeke's wife?'

'Yes, I am,' I said. 'Do you have a moment? I would like to

110

speak with you.' Something in my tone must have convinced her of my genuine concern for Helen.

'Why don't you come through that door over there, and I'll give you a nice glass of lemonade.'

'That would be very nice,' I said.

I followed the woman, who introduced herself as Mrs James, back into a small sitting room behind the post office. The corner had been converted to a kitchen area with an apartment-sized stove and refrigerator. A small table with two chairs sat under a window, overlooking Main Street.

'That corridor leads to my sitting area and the two bedrooms,' she said. 'The job includes a free place to live. After Mort died – that's my husband, god rest his soul – I needed a place. He left debts, and after they were paid, I didn't have much.' She smiled at me. 'But you didn't come to hear that, did you?'

'I think you know why I've come, Mrs James,' I said.

She busied herself in the tiny kitchen, and soon she set a tray down on the table, which held a pitcher of lemonade and a plate of homemade gingersnaps.

'Call me Maud. All my friends do.' She poured out lemonade and placed the cookies on the cut glass plates. 'Is it true that poor Ken was murdered by the same person who murdered Rachel all those years ago?'

'It's a possibility,' I said. 'I don't know much. Detective Bateson is handling the murder investigation and isn't forthcoming with details.'

'The cat burglar was the biggest news around. It's all people have been talking about for the past eight months or so. Now this. There are newspaper reporters everywhere. One of them came in here, my dear, and wanted me to tell them where you were staying.' She must have sensed my tension. 'Don't you worry, I didn't tell him.'

We ate in silence. I knew better than to rush Maud James with questions. I simply waited, knowing instinctively that she would speak when she was ready.

111

'I'm so glad you're here, Miss Sarah. The whole town is glad that Zeke has come home. And Miss Daphne must love having you around. She and Rachel were so close. She was devastated when Miss Rachel died. She needed another woman her own age. Miss Daphne, she's a beauty and holds herself real proper. And that sister of hers is a real firecracker, if you get my meaning. Anyone with a brain can see she and Joe Connor are meant for each other. Someone needs to get that child away from Arliss Winslow. And you must forgive me. I get a bit lonely since the husband died. Seem to have too much time on my hands. Thought about getting a cat – never mind, tell me, dear, what can I do for you?'

'I want to locate Helen,' I said.

She shook her head. 'I'm sorry. I gave my word.'

I set my glass down and pushed the plate of cookies away.

'Mrs James, I am going to trust you to keep what I'm about to say to you a secret. I believe Helen is in serious danger. I think she ran away because she saw something. I need to talk to her. I want to offer her money, so she can leave if she wants to. My husband can help her. Please. Tell me where she is. The police are looking for her, too. If they find her before I do, they will force her to come back.'

'Oh dear.' Mrs James had tied a gingham apron around her waist when she stepped into the kitchen. She clenched a piece of it in her hand now and twisted it. 'Oh dear.' She looked at me with worried eyes. 'I did give my word that I wouldn't tell anyone where she had gone.'

'I know you did, and if Helen wasn't in danger, I would respect that,' I said. 'But I think she has information about Rachel Caen's murder and Mr Connor's murder. She needs protection. I know you don't know me well, but I'm asking you to trust me.'

Worry etched Mrs James' face.

'I wouldn't ask if I didn't need to,' I repeated myself, in an effort to convince Mrs James to break her vow of silence.

With a sigh the woman spoke. 'She's at her sister's in Chesterton. I'll give you the address, but you must promise that you'll protect her. I trust Zeke. If anyone can keep her safe, he can.'

Fifteen minutes later, I walked out of the post office with Helen Dicks's location in my pocketbook. My mind was busy calculating how I could escape Zeke's meddling family long enough to look for Helen, when I stepped onto the sidewalk and collided with Nick Newland.

Chapter 12

My purse went sprawling. Its contents spilled onto the sidewalk. I bent to pick up the lipstick, compact, hairpins, handkerchief, and pencils that were scattered about. Maybe if I ignored Nick, he would go away. No such luck. I stuffed everything into my pocketbook and stood up.

'You dropped this.' He handed me the sterling compact. I reached for it, but Nick held it just out of reach. 'Not quite. You're going to tell me about the emeralds.'

'What are you talking about?'

'Don't play coy with me, Sarah. I know that the emeralds, allegedly lost when Rachel Caen died, are starting to surface. I want to know why. I want to know if they are connected with her death, and I want to know if she was murdered.'

'So you're going to hold my compact hostage until I answer your questions?'

'Of course not.' He handed me the compact, which I snatched out of his hand and stuffed safely in my purse.

'Good day, Mr Newland.' I couldn't get away fast enough.

He moved so he blocked my way on the sidewalk.

'Not so fast. I think we should go have a cup of coffee or maybe a sandwich. You see, Sarah, I suggest you tell me what you know. Don't worry. I'll protect your identity. I'm quite fastidious about protecting my sources, but you will talk to me because if you don't, I'll write a story about you, about your past, about your time in the asylum, and how you accused your adoptive father of murder.'

'Mr Newland, I won't be bullied into doing something against my will. I don't care what you write,' I said.

'No problem,' Nick said. 'It's nice to see you.'

I watched him hurry away, puzzled at his sudden change in attitude.

'I think I may have scared him,' a voice said behind me. Wade Connor stood on the sidewalk, a sheepish smile on his face. 'Mr Newland doesn't much care for me.'

'What are you doing here?' I asked before I realized that Wade had come home to attend his father's funeral. 'I'm sorry about your father, Wade. I only met him once, but he seemed a decent man.'

'I didn't mean to surprise you.' Wade stood in the blazing heat dressed in a navy wool suit, complete with a white button-up shirt and tie. He didn't even break a sweat. 'I've come to fetch you. I went to the house, and they said you had gone walking. Zeke's going to meet us there.'

'What's going on? Why have you come to get me? Is Zeke okay?'

'He's fine. If you don't mind, I'd prefer to wait and speak to you and Zeke together, so I don't have to repeat myself.' He looked at me out of the corner of his eyes. 'You seem to have settled in quite well. I'm impressed that Mrs James took you into her private apartment. She doesn't do that for everyone.'

'You've been following me?'

'I simply walked behind you. You didn't notice me, so I decided to see where you went.' He led me to his car, and once we were situated, sped off at breakneck speed. Wade didn't speak during the ride home. His eyes kept darting to the rearview mirror, and he clutched the steering wheel in a white-knuckled grip. I couldn't shake the sensation that something was very wrong.

* * *

The house looked forlorn and empty. The only sign of life was the bumblebees, who floated lazily among the flowers in the garden. Wade came around and opened my door for me. When I got out of the car, he placed a protective hand on the small of my back as he surveyed the surroundings.

'Let's get you inside,' he said. We hurried up the front steps and headed toward the study. We found Zeke sitting with his bad leg propped up on an ottoman, an empty glass in his hand, his head tipped back, and his eyes closed in repose. Wade and I stood for a moment, watching Zeke as he sat still, oblivious of our presence.

'Zeke,' Wade said.

My husband woke up, startled. When he saw Wade, he stood up. The two men shook hands.

'Sorry about your pop,' Zeke said.

'I know. Me too,' Wade said.

'Want a refill?' I ignored Wade and nodded at the glass in Zeke's hand.

'Yes,' Zeke said.

I took the empty glass and headed over to the sideboard that held the spirits. Someone had put fresh ice in the bucket.

'Better pour one for all of us,' Wade said. I poured a healthy dose of scotch over ice into two of the glasses, and opted for a plain soda water for myself. Once we were settled, drinks in hand, Wade, who now sat on the sofa opposite Zeke, spoke.

'Another emerald has turned up, in Seattle this time. They're trying to trace it. We must acknowledge that whoever murdered my father in all likelihood murdered Rachel,' Wade said. 'And, as you both know, Simon is the most likely candidate, at least according to Detective Bateson. We all know that Simon isn't capable of murdering a fly. I cannot believe that fool, Bateson, has risen to the rank of detective.'

'What about tracing the most recent emerald? Someone had to sell it. Can't you find out who that person is?' Zeke asked.

'I can only hope that Detective Bateson is taking advantage of the FBI's offer to help. Since my father is the victim, I can't—'

The front door opened and shut. Familiar footsteps echoed in the hallway. Wade jumped up, pulled the gun out of the holster in his jacket, and crept over to the door.

'It's just Daphne,' I said. 'What's going on? You're wound up so tight, you're giving me a headache. You're keeping something from us. What is it?'

Wade tucked the gun out of sight and sat back down.

'Wade?' Zeke's voice had an edge to it.

'There was a fire,' Wade said. He stood up and walked to the window. He stood with his back to us, fidgeting with the change in his pants pocket.

'Where?' Zeke's voice cut.

'Sausalito. Your home. I'm afraid it's gone. I'm sorry. I really am.'

'What the devil do you mean?' Zeke snapped. 'You were to keep an eye on things. You assured me that you would keep my home safe. Are you saying that one of Hendrik Shrader's henchmen got past your men and burned my house down? What in god's name do you have to say for yourself? How in the hell did you let this happen? I cannot even believe this.' Zeke was shouting now.

'Our house?' My voice came in a whisper. The tears welled in my eyes and dripped down my cheek. I didn't bother to stop them. 'Was anyone hurt?'

'No,' Wade said. 'No casualties. No fatalities.'

'You know how difficult it is to find a place to live in Marin County or the City for that matter? What are we supposed to do?' Zeke stood up now, too. I had never seen him this angry before. 'It just never ends. I cannot have any peace.'

I thought of the furniture that we had bought together for our new home, the happy hours we had spent deciding what went where. I thought of Zeke, clad in an apron, in our tiny kitchen making some precise sauce to put atop our fish. Gone. Reduced to ashes.

'You know full well that you can't just step out of the life you've been living without repercussions. You've made enemies, Zeke. You'll need diligence for the rest of your life. You know that. Sarah knows that. But never mind. I'll personally find you another place to live when you're ready to come home.' Wade refilled his glass and Zeke's before he sat back down. 'You've every right to be furious with me. I will make this right with you, on my honor. But Nick Newland is in town. He cornered Sarah today. Right now I need to focus on keeping him quiet.'

'I want protection for Sarah,' Zeke said. 'You can't keep our presence here a secret forever. I demand that you assume that Hendrik Shrader knows where we are.'

'It's done. There are men in place now.' Wade looked at me. 'I've six men on the perimeter of the house. They will be there around the clock. If you want an agent inside, I can do that, too.'

'That's not necessary,' I said. 'I'll keep the doors locked. You've got the exterior covered. That should be sufficient.'

'Sarah—' Zeke started to speak.

'No. I don't want to upset the others. I'll stay locked in the house unless you are with me. Daphne, Granna, Simon, and Toby don't need to know about Hendrik Shrader.' I looked at Wade. 'Just make sure no harm comes to them, Wade. Promise me you'll keep them safe.'

'I promise,' Wade said.

'What about Newland?'

'I am going to bribe him,' Wade said.

'With what?' I asked.

118

'I'm going to promise him an exclusive on the murder investigation, as long as he doesn't publish anything until the case is resolved. I've already arranged it with Bateson. Now I just need to convince Mr Newland.' Wade finished his drink and stood up. 'I was just going to discuss the logistics of my plan with him now.'

'I'm coming with you,' Zeke said. 'In case he needs some extra persuading.'

Zeke kissed my cheek and left me on the couch, numb and frightened, images of our house – now reduced to cinders – floating around in my head.

* * *

The next morning, Zeke insisted that I learn to use my gun. And rather than have an FBI agent with me at all times, I capitulated. We set out early for the old barn, in an attempt to beat the heat. Neither one of us spoke of Hendrik Shrader, Simon, or Ken Connor's murder.

'Your leg seems better today,' I said.

'The exercise seems to help.' He took a deep breath. 'It should rain soon.'

'But there's not a cloud in the sky.'

'Trust me, my love. The rain is coming.'

Zeke brought ear protection for both of us. 'Wear these, or your ears will ring for hours, my love. No need to suffer.' He set a series of tin cans on the picnic table in a clean, even line. We spent a few minutes going over safety issues. Zeke showed me the proper way to stand, hold the gun, and how to sight my target.

'When you shoot this, it's going to be loud, so prepare yourself. Don't pull the trigger,' he said. 'Just squeeze it with your finger.'

I did as he instructed. I lined up the sight and squeezed. The loud boom of the shot reverberated. Birds flew from the trees. Horses took off running, the sound of galloping hooves reverberating through the ground beneath us.

'I've woken up the neighborhood,' I said.

'You missed,' Zeke said. 'Try again. Just line the sight of the gun and focus on those cans.'

I tried again. And missed again.

'It'd help if she'd open her eyes,' Daphne said. She strode through the tall grass toward us, a teasing smile on her face. 'And she needs to relax her shoulders. Sarah, don't think so much.' She pulled a pair of ear protectors out of the rucksack she carried and placed them on her head. Then she took the gun from me, faced the cans, and positioned her feet so they were shoulder width apart. She pulled the trigger and hit the can dead on.

'Very good, Daph,' Zeke said.

'Don't worry, Sarah. It takes practice.' She used her hand to shield her eyes as she tipped her head back, looking at the barn. 'This place is a hazard.'

'It really is,' Zeke said.

'Add it to the list of things to deal with,' Daphne said. 'Zeke, I've come to tell you that you're wanted at the mill. Simon says to come right away.' She helped us gather up the tin cans and stow the ear protectors back in the car. I put my gun back in the case. We walked back to the house, enjoying the cool morning air.

'Simon told me about your home. I hope you'll both consider staying here. You know you're welcome.'

'Thanks,' I said.

'We really can't make any plans yet,' Zeke said. 'We're certainly going to stay until the mill is back up and running.'

Once we got back to the house, Zeke changed into work clothes, kissed my cheek, and left me with Daphne. We sat together at a table on the patio, enjoying the last vestige of crisp morning air. In another half an hour, it would be hot. Again.

'Do you want to go riding?' Daphne asked. 'I've a horse that's as gentle as can be.'

'Oh, I don't ride,' I said.

'No, really, this horse is the equivalent of sitting in a chair.' Daphne smiled at me.

'I have so much work. Can I take a rain check?'

'Of course.' Daphne folded the newspaper she had been reading and tucked it under her plate, arranging it just so. With a sigh, she moved it to the vacant chair between us. 'Sarah, are you going to look for Helen?'

'I don't know how I would go about that,' I said. 'If she needs to be found, I'm sure the police will find her.'

'No good can come from meddling, Sarah. If I were you, I'd leave her be,' Daphne said. I didn't speak. I didn't want to lie to Daphne, but I also didn't want her to know that I had every intention of finding Helen.

'Okay. I'm off to the stables,' Daphne said. We said our good-byes, and Daphne headed to the barn, walking in long strides.

Back in my room, another huge bouquet of flowers, arranged in yet another stunning vase, sat on the small table in front of the sofa. A simple note written in Daphne's handwriting accompanied the arrangement: '*So sorry to hear about your home in Sausalito. I hope you know you have a home here. In fond friendship, Daphne.*'

Daphne was trying to be my friend, and it seemed that I rebuffed her at every turn. I vowed to make an effort.

Chapter 13

Two days passed before I was able to go to Chesterton to see Helen. Dr Geisler sent me a packet of handwritten notes to transcribe, but there was no usual cover letter with this batch, only a single page with the word RUSH scrawled across the top in his handwriting. I spent my days working, while Zeke spent his at the mill, working at a fever pitch to reopen on schedule.

The newspapers reported the RAF and the Yanks were in the fourth night of an all-out assault on the Reich. The meat and butter shortage continued, Emil Ludwig predicted that Hitler would soon be assassinated, and the Millport Climber continued to outfox the police. Every night another house was burgled. The stories became more and more outlandish, as the Climber's behavior escalated.

One morning, right after Zeke and Simon left for the mill, I slipped out of the house, decked out in hat, gloves, and a light coat, despite the blazing heat. Certain that no one had followed me, I caught the nine o'clock train to Chesterton and spent the two-hour train trip trying to focus on the pile of newspapers I had grabbed before I left the house. The headlines were bleak: GERMAN PRISONERS AT ANGEL ISLAND ARE SURE OF GERMAN VICTORY! Next to that, a City of Paris ad encouraged shoppers to purchase their springtime dresses for children. When an article by Mrs Pinkerton – whoever she may be – about using corn flakes to extend meat rations made my eyelids go heavy, I stuffed the newspapers into my purse and watched the countryside go by.

I stepped off the train at 11.05 a.m., stuffed my coat, gloves, and hat in a locker at the station, and headed out onto the street. Chesterton and Millport were both small towns, but Millport had the mill, and all the employees needed for its increased wartime production. Millport bustled with life. The sidewalks were always full of people. The restaurants always with a queue for a table. Chesterton, on the other hand, seemed bucolic and untouched. There was once a coffee shop at the station, but it had a sign in the window announcing that it was closed until further notice. I was the only person to exit the train. Lucky for me, a lone taxi cab stood on the curb.

'One-twenty Maple,' I said to the driver.

He didn't say a word, just drove for about five minutes, turning on a road that was lined in neat little cottages, most of them whitewashed stucco. I paid his fare and dismissed him, knowing that I would swelter on the walk back to the station, but I didn't care.

The house, like all the others, had a trim lawn in the front. A brick walkway led up to a spacious porch, with a swing on one side. Helen sat on the swing, her feet curled up underneath her, reading a book. When she saw me, she shut the book and laid it down next to her.

'What are you doing here? You haven't told anyone where I am, have you?'

'Of course not,' I said.

'Were you followed?' She got up from the swing and surveyed the street. Satisfied that no one else had followed me, she sat back down. 'I don't mean to be rude, Miss Sarah, but you've no business here. How did you find me?'

123

'Never mind that,' I said. 'No one at the house knows I'm here, and I have no intention of telling anyone. I came because I want to help you.'

'Simon didn't kill anyone. I'm sure of it. And that's all I'm saying.'

'Helen, you realize that if Simon is found guilty of murder, he could hang,' I said.

'He won't be found guilty because he didn't do anything. You and Zeke will fix it.' She started to gnaw her fingernail, realized what she was doing, and sat on her hands.

'But what if we can't?'

'You can. Zeke will take care of it. He and Wade Connor are very powerful men. They won't let anything happen to Simon.'

'Helen, why won't you go to the police? Tell them what you saw. Tell them what you're afraid of. Zeke and Joe can keep you safe.'

Tears welled up in her eyes. She wiped them with the back of her sleeve before she shook her head. 'This isn't about staying safe. I don't care about me. This isn't about me. I'm not talking to anyone. You shouldn't have come. Please go.'

Her words were sharp and hurtful, but an underlying tone of desperation hung between us. 'Simon will be okay.' Her voice was soft now, defeated. 'I trust Joe Connor. He's a good cop.'

'Joe Connor is not allowed to work the case, Helen. It's a conflict of interest. Detective Bateson has been assigned to the case, and he hates Simon.'

'Please go.' She wiped the tears from her cheeks as she got up from the swing and stood facing the street, her back to me. 'Please leave.'

* * *

The sweat had soaked through my dress by the time I got back to the station. Defeated, I settled into my seat and closed my eyes.

Soon the motion of the train rocked me to sleep, and the two hours zipped by. A hand on my arm awoke me with a start.

'Ma'am.' The conductor smiled at me and spoke in a gentle voice. 'I believe your stop is coming up.'

'Thanks,' I said, sitting up, surprised that I had slept so long. He nodded and moved down the aisle. The nap served me well. I de-trained rested and refreshed and ready for the next impending disaster.

I had half a mind to call the house and ask for someone to come and pick me up, but changed my mind when I thought of all the questions I would have to answer. I didn't want anyone at the house – other than Zeke – to know I had found Helen, so I braved the heat and started the long walk home, sticking to the shaded lanes, not caring that my shoes were getting ruined by the dirt roads. The solitude of the summer day lulled me. The bees buzzed, birds swished in the brush, and the grass waved in sweet golden waves. I savored it all, until a cloak of silence fell over me. The birds stopped singing, even the breeze stopped. Gauging the abandoned barn was just around the corner, I stopped, listening for footsteps.

When I heard them, I stepped off the road and crept in silence until the barn came into view. Staying out of sight, I watched someone whose face I couldn't see, nimble and spry as a schoolboy, duck into the barn. Whoever it was carried a rucksack, similar to the one which I had found in Simon's desk. He was dressed in an untucked baggy shirt, which hung down to his knees. A baseball hat and aviator glasses prevented me from seeing his face or his hair. He ducked into the barn and came out a few seconds later, emptyhanded. I waited, hidden in the bushes, not daring to breathe, until he scurried off. Then I waited some more – just in case he changed his mind and came back – before I went to the barn.

Sunlight filtered through the gaps in the rotted wood, showing the dust that floated in the air. The smell of rotten hay and mildew assaulted me. I held my nose, so as not to sneeze. After my eyes adjusted to the light, I searched. I found the rucksack stashed behind a pile of rotten wood, the only hiding place available.

I opened the rucksack and gasped. Even in the dull light of the barn, the silver glistened and gleamed. There was a candelabra and silver flatware – salad forks, dessert forks, knives, spoons, teaspoons, soup spoons. By my quick count, the rucksack held service for sixteen people.

I had found the Millport Climber's stash for the second time.

* * *

Zeke and Joe were standing in front of the house as I came running up.

'Don't go anywhere,' I said to both of them. I dumped my purse, coat, and hat in the foyer, and hurried back down to the driveway where the men stood before Joe's car. 'Come with me, please.' I got in the backseat of the car. 'We need to go to the old barn.' Both men stood there, staring at me. 'Now. Please.'

Zeke moved first. He hurried around to the front of the car. Soon Joe followed suit and we were on our way.

'Would you care to tell us why we are rushing to the abandoned barn?' Zeke finally asked.

'I've found the Climber's stash,' I said.

Zeke drove as fast as the conditions on the dirt road allowed. We skidded to a halt and sat for a moment in a cloud of dust. Joe grabbed a flashlight from the glovebox, jumped out of the car, and propped the barn door open with a piece of wood, allowing maximum light in.

'This place really needs to be torn down,' he called to us over his shoulder.

'It's on the list of things do,' Zeke responded. He came around the back and offered me his hand. 'Are you okay?'

'Just hot. Had a bit of a grueling day.'

126

He kissed my sweaty cheek and together we followed Joe into the dank building.

Joe stood in the center of the barn, shining light into corners that had been dark for decades. 'It's over here,' I said. They followed me to the pile of rotten lumber. I reached into the space and felt around for the sack. It was gone.

Joe and Zeke tore through the whole pile of wood, moving the boards that didn't disintegrate. They found nothing.

'Are you sure of what you saw?' Joe said.

'Of course, I'm sure. I touched it. It was right there.'

'Someone's been here.' Zeke pointed to the footprints in the dust.

'Tell me everything that happened,' Joe said.

'I was walking down the lane. The birds and bees were busy, and there was that general hum. Then it stopped. Everything grew silent. That's what caught my attention. It seemed as though I wasn't alone. I don't know what made me step off the path, but I did, and I hid in the bushes. A person came through the grassy area, over the knoll. He wore a hat, an oversized shirt, and baggy trousers.'

'A disguise?' Zeke asked.

'Well, I couldn't recognize him, so I would say yes. He went into the barn, but when he came out he didn't have the rucksack.' I opened my eyes now. 'So I went in to see what was in it.'

'That's wonderful, my love,' Zeke said. He smiled at me.

'Does she always act so impetuously?' Joe asked.

'She does,' Zeke said. 'That's part of her charm.' Joe shook his head.

'I heard you went to Chesterton today. You didn't stay long,' Joe said.

'How did you know that?'

Neither Joe nor Zeke spoke.

'You had me followed?' I spoke to Joe. 'Did you know that he had me followed?' I all but shouted at Zeke, not caring that Joe was

127

there to bear witness. 'I promised I would keep her whereabouts a secret. I cannot believe you would betray me like that.'

Zeke moved close, as if to take me in his arms. I stepped away.

'Don't blame him, Sarah. It was Detective Bateson. He realized that Helen might have some important information after all, and he suspected you would lead him to her.'

'If Detective Bateson shows up at her house, she'll never forgive me. She'll never trust me again,' I said.

'If Detective Bateson brings Helen back to town, I give you my word that she will stay safe,' Zeke said.

'How can you guarantee that?'

'I'm going to help him,' Joe said. 'This is partially her fault. If she had come forward right away, we wouldn't be in this position. She brought it on herself. Did she tell you what she saw?'

I shook my head. 'No. She's not going to tell anyone. What if she saw who put the rucksack in Simon's room? What if the person is someone important? It will be her word against theirs. Who do you think will be believed? Helen will be dismissed as unreliable. After all, she's just a woman, right? It's not like she has any social standing in the community. She'll still be in danger, and now, since the police have no use of her, they won't protect her.'

'That's not going to happen,' Zeke said. 'I'll bring her to our house if I have to.'

I wanted to run back to the house, away from Zeke and Joe, but I was too hot, and my feet were killing me from the two mile walk home. What I needed, what I craved, was a big glass of water and a cold bath.

* * *

Detective Bateson and a uniformed police officer were waiting by the front door when we arrived at the house. The detective blocked my door, all but preventing me from exiting the car. 'You're the one I want to speak with. Get out here. Now.'

128

'Get away from the car, Bateson,' Zeke said. 'She's going to rest. You can see her tomorrow morning.'

I do love my husband, I thought. He came around to my side of the car, careful to position his body between Detective Bateson and me.

'Your wife went to see her friend Helen today, and now the girl has disappeared.'

'What happened? Where did she go?'

Detective Bateson looked at Zeke, as if waiting for a man, or someone with some authority over me, to take over. Zeke didn't say a word. Joe leaned against the car, the telltale signs of a smile etched into the corner of his mouth. I liked Joe just then. I liked him just fine.

'We don't know. After you left the house, one of my officers went to get her. She was gone.'

'So you lost her?' Joe said.

'I need your help finding her.'

'Why didn't you listen to me yesterday?' I asked.

'You shouldn't have let your wife get involved, Zeke. Surely you can control her,' Detective Bateson said.

'Bateson, you have absolutely no understanding of women. God help the one who marries you,' Zeke said.

'We should help him,' Joe said, 'for Helen's sake. She's not safe out there alone.'

'We'll find her. She's an ignorant girl. How far do you think she can get? Once we find her, we'll keep her in protective custody,' Detective Bateson said.

'You will do no such thing. She's going to stay in my care,' Zeke said.

'But—'

'Don't. Just don't. I've just about had it with you.'

'Let's meet at the station in half an hour,' Joe said, all but ignoring Detective Bateson. 'We can figure out what resources we have and how best to use them.'

129

'Now listen here, Connor. This is my investigation—'

'Half an hour,' Joe said to Zeke. He got behind the wheel of Detective Bateson's car. 'Wait a second, Connor,' Detective Bateson said. He opened the door and managed to scramble in, just as Joe Connor pulled away.

'I don't think you should come with us,' Zeke said. He expected me to argue, demand that I be able to join them as they searched for Helen. But I didn't have the strength, and I knew full well that I would just be a source of worry for Zeke and Joe.

'You'll find her, won't you?'

The look in Zeke's eyes spoke a thousand words, but he didn't respond to my question. My husband didn't make promises that he couldn't keep.

'I'll be back as soon as I can.' He kissed my cheek and was gone.

Craving privacy and some time away from all the Caen family drama, I stepped into the cool darkness of our bedroom. Not bothering to turn on the light, I kicked off my shoes, slipped my dress over my head, and left it in a filthy heap on the floor. I sat down on the sofa and was slipping off my stockings when there was a knock at the door. I thought about ignoring whoever it was, but Daphne barged in. I bit back my resentment when I saw that she carried a tray with a pitcher of lemonade and a plate of sandwiches. I hadn't eaten all day. The food and drink were a welcome sight indeed.

'I'm sorry to barge in,' she said.

I flipped on the lamp and made a spot for the tray on the coffee table.

'Thanks.' Daphne set the tray down and poured me a glass of lemonade.

'I saw you walk up the driveway and get in the car with Zeke and Joe. Where did you go?' I didn't want to answer questions right now. I didn't want to deal with Daphne, even though she had come to me in friendship.

'You're exhausted. I didn't mean to pry,' she said.

'It's okay,' I said. 'I am so hot. It's been a long day.'

'Where did you go?'

'I took the train to Chesterton,' I said. 'Dr Geisler needed me to speak to someone there to verify a few things on the manuscript I am working on.'

'Chesterton? That seems like an awful long way.'

'It was, but the man helped me, and my employer will be happy with the results of my trip.'

'I so admire you for your career. I hope you realize how lucky you are to have so much independence. Do you mind?' She pointed to the second glass on the tray.

'Not at all,' I lied. I went into the bathroom, turned on the water to fill the tub, tied my dressing gown over my slip, and joined Daphne in the sitting room.

'Are you and Zeke going to have children?' she asked

'Haven't given it much thought,' I said, another lie. 'At some point, we are going to have to deal with our mess in Sausalito. Our house, the insurance, all that awaits us when we return home.'

'So you don't think you'll stay here?'

'Zeke will stay until things are sorted.' I set my empty glass down, looked longingly at the bathtub and hoped Daphne would take the hint.

'I'm sorry for you, Sarah.' She stood and gave me a quick hug. 'I'm here, if you want to talk, or if I can do anything.'

'That means a lot, Daphne. Thanks.'

'See you at dinner.' She let herself out the door. After her footsteps faded away, I locked the door against other intruders and got into the tub.

An hour later, I emerged cleansed of dust and sweat and the events of the day. I poured myself another glass of lemonade, not caring that the ice had melted it into water, and drank it slowly. I opened the wardrobe and selected a turquoise linen dress that I would wear down to dinner. I had one box of stockings left and wondered if I would ever again be able to get this fine silk, sheer and thin as a butterfly's wings. I moved over to the dresser and opened the drawer where my slips and camisoles had been arranged into symmetrical piles by Helen. The space where the box that contained my pearl necklace and earrings should have lain stood bare. Frantic, I rifled through the drawer. The pearls were gone. Someone had stolen my jewelry.

Chapter 14

I tore apart my dresser, tossing my clothes on the floor, not caring where they landed. The pearls were gone. The fountain pen was gone. My house was gone. Zeke found me sitting in a puddle of sunlight, the drawers from my dresser, along with the clothes that they held, scattered around me.

He held out a hand and hoisted me to my feet, enveloping me in a hug with one motion. 'What's happened?'

'The Climber stole my pearls and my fountain pen,' I said, 'and I have nothing of my past. My entire life – our life – is in ashes in Sausalito. The only jewelry I own has been stolen. The pen has been stolen.'

'I see you've conducted a diligent search,' Zeke said. 'Do you want help putting your clothes away?'

'What are we going to do? Where are we going to live? Are we going back to Sausalito?'

'What do you want to do?' He brushed my cheek with his fingers.

I paused a moment, surveying the wreckage of my room.

'Find Helen, exonerate Simon,' I said. 'It's hard to make plans with those two things hanging over our heads.'

'I think I may be required to stay here for at least a month or two. Simon needs my help. After we deal with the legal issues, he is going to need me to help get the mill up and running to full efficiency. But never mind that. I'll leave tomorrow if you want.'

'Really?'

'Yes, really. We'll find a place to live that we both like. No need for anyone to be miserable.'

'You're so logical,' I said.

'And you're so emotional.' He kissed my forehead. 'We don't have to decide anything right now. Why don't we just stay here until it's time to go, and trust that we'll know when that is.'

He led me to the sofa. We sat down next to each other. A breeze came through the open window. The curtain undulated, like a wave. Thunder rumbled in the distance, a portent of rain and the promise of a break in the heat. I shut my eyes and leaned my head back. Something niggled at the back of my mind, and just like that, the missing piece clicked into place.

'Oh.' I stood up, walked to the window. 'I cannot believe I didn't figure it out sooner.'

'You – what?'

'The way she moves. I'd have recognized that nimble gait of hers anywhere. What a blind fool I've been.'

'Sarah, my love, what are you talking about?'

'Sophie,' I said. 'It's Sophie. I can't believe I didn't see it sooner. Sophie Winslow is the Millport Climber.'

'Sophie? That is totally absurd,' Zeke said. 'I've known that girl my whole life—'

'And that, dear husband, is your problem. You have this preconceived idea of who she is based on your knowledge of her as a child. Put yourself in her shoes for a minute. She has absolutely no freedom. Her mother bullies her in public. Arliss slapped her as though she were an aberrant teenager. How old is Sophie? Twenty-six? Twenty-seven? And she just kowtows to her mother. Arliss won't let her go anywhere, do anything, or have any freedom.' I watched Zeke, gauging his reaction to my words. 'You and I have both said that the Climber is doing this for thrills, and that's why the heists are getting riskier and riskier. Think about it. It makes sense, doesn't it?'

'Good god,' Zeke said. I waited for him to absorb my words. 'Your assumptions are sound, if looked at from a certain perspective. Let's say you're right, for argument's sake. What do we do? Call Joe? Do you want Sophie to go to jail?'

'No. I don't think she deserves that,' I said.

'Listen to yourself,' Zeke said. He unlaced his shoes before he kicked them off and put his feet on the coffee table.

'I'm well aware of what I'm saying,' I said.

'Sarah, you don't get to decide the punishment for people who have committed crimes. It doesn't work that way. If – and this is a big if – Sophie is indeed the Climber, she will need to pay the price, like all other criminals. Granted, her mother will probably get her a good lawyer, just because she will have no stomach for the scandal that will go along with Sophie's arrest.'

'Poor Sophie,' I said.

'What do you mean, poor Sophie? That girl has been nothing but rude to you since we got here.'

'I know, but after witnessing the way Arliss treats her – I'd rather be an orphan than have a mother like Arliss Winslow. Can we just leave the police out of it? What if she gives everything back?'

Zeke laughed out loud.

'No, we can't do that. Let's tell Wade what we suspect. Let him handle it. He's the master at making problems go away.'

'You're brilliant,' I said, planting a kiss on his lips. I smiled at the thought of Arliss Winslow and Wade Connor going to battle over Sophie.

My money was on Wade, no question.

* * *

The thunder rumbled, but the rain didn't come. The locals waited for the deluge with a calm patience born of experience. Not me. I suffered and took cold baths to ease my pain. Thursday morning dawned as hot as ever.

Zeke had gone downstairs to fetch our tray of coffee, toast, and fresh marmalade. He poured his coffee and took it into the bath, where he splashed in the water, singing in a fine baritone.

Nick Newland's article appeared on the front page of the morning paper: MILLPORT MURDER TIED TO 1939 SUICIDE! CASE REOPENED. FOUL PLAY SUSPECTED – MILLPORT PD STUMPED!

I tossed the paper aside and had just sat down at my desk, when Wade Connor walked into the sitting room, rapping on the door as he pushed his way in.

'Good thing I'm dressed,' I said. 'What are you doing here? It's only eight o'clock.'

'Good morning to you, too. Zeke called and asked me to come. He said there was something you wanted to talk to me about. I can come back,' he said.

'Good morning.' Zeke came out of the bathroom in a cloud of steam, buttoning his shirt as he walked. 'Coffee?'

'No, thanks.' And in that manner that belonged to Wade exclusively, we got down to business. 'What's going on?'

'I think I'm going to let Sarah explain,' Zeke said.

'Sarah? Why do I get the feeling I'm not going to like this?' Wade sat down on the chair next to the sofa. I glanced at Rachel's portrait. She stared down at me, strong and sure.

'I think Sophie Winslow is the Millport Climber,' I said. When Wade started to huff and puff, I interrupted. 'Just wait, Wade, please. Listen.'

'Fine.' He took the cup on the tray that was intended for me. 'Go ahead.'

I told him what I thought, explained the reasoning behind my theory. I told him of the encounter I witnessed between Sophie and her mother on the night of the party. 'It was something about the carriage of her shoulders, and the way she looked side to side before she entered the building. It was Sophie. I'm sure of it.'

'We don't think she had anything to do with Rachel's murder or the theft of the emeralds,' Zeke said.

'Then how did the emeralds wind up in Simon's desk?' Wade asked.

'We don't know,' Zeke and I said at the same time.

'You two are just a regular vaudeville act, aren't you? If this is true, if Sophie really is the Climber, Arliss Winslow will make everyone's life miserable. You realize that, of course. I'm guessing that's why you called me.' Wade had the grace to laugh. 'I've always loathed that woman. And I know firsthand that she treats Sophie reprehensibly.' He stood up. 'Thanks for telling me. Let me think about it. I'll talk to Joe, and we'll figure something out.' Zeke and Wade shook hands. Wade nodded at me and let himself out the door.

'Well, at least we don't have to deal with that,' Zeke said. He kissed my cheek and breezed out the door, leaving me to the stack of handwritten notes and the typewriter.

I forced myself to sit down at my desk and work, but couldn't shake my ever increasing worry about Helen. When I made the same typo for the fourth time, I pushed away from the desk, wanting to do something productive, but not sure what that something was. Rachel stared down at me from her portrait, taunting me from her lofty position above the fireplace.

'What should I do?' I said. 'Show me what to do.' My voice echoed in the stillness. Rachel didn't answer me.

'Fine,' I said. 'I'm going for a walk.'

I headed out into the morning sunshine, breathing in the fresh air and making a concerted effort to ignore the FBI men that were entrenched at various positions around the property. Two of them followed me as I headed down the path to the woods. I planned on circling the lake and heading home, a respectable distance which should clear the cobwebs. Things were coming to a head here in Millport. I knew that once Wade Connor made it known that Sophie was the Climber, Arliss Winslow would be on the warpath. It wouldn't take her long to discover that I was responsible for the revelation of her daughter's malfeasance. She would be furious with me, of that I was certain. She would set out to discredit me and ruin me socially. Arliss Winslow's wrath didn't bother me. Social ruin in the town didn't bother me, either.

By the time I'd walked the circumference of the lake and headed back to the house, my head was clear, my step purposeful. I nodded at the two FBI men who had followed me around the lake. They wore suits and ties and were both wringing wet with sweat.

'If you come in, I'll give you some lemonade,' I called out.

'No, thanks, ma'am. You go on in.' They waved at me and took their places in the shade under some trees.

I met Mrs Griswold in the hall carrying a basket of Toby's clothes, the majority of them covered with dust and grime, to the washing machine in the basement.

'He's a sweet boy, but if there is dirt, he will be in it.' She smiled at me.

'Mrs Griswold, can you see that the FBI men get something cold to drink? I asked them to come in, but they refused.'

'Of course,' she said. 'I'll see to it right away. Did you go out the back door when you left for your walk?'

'No. I went out the front. Why?'

Mrs Griswold furrowed her brow and shook her head. 'It's strange. I thought I heard footsteps and a door closing. I've searched the house. All the doors are locked and there's not a soul here, except the two of us. No one could have got past those agents outside.' She shrugged her shoulders. 'Probably my imagination.'

Mrs Griswold and I had only known each other for a short time, but she did not strike me as someone who saw things that weren't there.

'Do you think we should have one of the agents come in and double check the house?' I asked.

She shook her head. 'No. It's nothing, I'm sure.'

The minute I let myself into my room I sensed my heartbeat was not the only one in the room. I closed the door behind me and stood silent, daring not to breathe. As Zeke instructed, my gun lay at the ready in my desk drawer. I kicked off my shoes, so as not to make any noise, and retrieved it. I held it with a shaking hand and moved into the bathroom. I swished the shower curtain aside. No one. I opened the curtains to reveal the bay window. No one. I tiptoed into my bedroom, stopping short when I saw the figure lying on my bed. I pointed the gun with a shaking hand just as the person snored and turned on her side to face me.

Helen. Fast asleep on my bed.

Chapter 15

'Helen.' I moved toward her. She didn't respond. I reached out to touch her shoulder. Just before my hand made contact, she snored again, a deep, nasal grunt. She slept on, unaware of my presence. Her brown lace-up shoes lay next to my bed, scuffed and soiled. The soles were worn all the way through in places. She hadn't bothered to take off her stockings; both of them were torn with ladders up the sides and gaping holes in the heels. Blisters had formed on both of her big toes. One of them had bled and scabbed over. She stank of sweat, and dirt, and fear. Her dress had stains in the armpits, as though she had been running and sweating for a long time. I should have woken her and demanded an explanation, but I didn't have the heart. At least she was safe. No one would think to look for her here. I would have to hide her and keep her safe until Zeke got home. I hoped that my husband could make Helen see reason. I went back into the sitting room and turned the key in the lock.

Knowing that Mrs Griswold would be in the basement dealing with Toby's laundry, I hurried downstairs and assembled a tray of bread, butter, jam, a pitcher of water, a pot of coffee, and the last of a wheel of cheddar cheese. If she asked, I would tell

140

Mrs Griswold that I had helped myself to a snack. She might wonder at my sudden appetite, but she wouldn't mention it to anyone.

'Helen,' I shook her shoulder. 'Wake up.'

She yelped and sat up, her eyes wide with terror. 'You're safe.' I pointed to the tray. 'Are you hungry?'

'Starved,' she said. 'I haven't eaten in hours, and I've come ever so far.'

'Did you walk here?'

'Part of the way,' she said. 'I'm in trouble, Sarah.'

'I know. I want to help you. Eat first, my dear. I'll get you some clean clothes and we'll figure out what to do.'

'Thanks. I should have listened to you from the beginning. If I had gone to Zeke when I first—'

'That doesn't matter. You're here now. I'll keep you safe.'

After she finished eating, Helen ran herself a bath while I surveyed my clothes, trying to find something that would fit. Helen hadn't brought anything with her except her handbag, and the clothes that she wore were beyond repair. Just then, a voice carried through the door.

'Sarah? Can I come in?'

I ran into the bathroom, slamming the door shut behind me. Helen sat neck deep in bubbles, her eyes wide.

'I'm in the tub,' I called out.

'Oh.' There was a question in Daphne's tone. I imagined her, standing outside my door, her head cocked, wondering what had possessed me to take my bath now. 'Well, lunch will be ready in fifteen minutes.'

'Okay, thanks.'

I tiptoed over to the door and kept my ear pressed against it until Daphne's footsteps faded away. Back in the bathroom, Helen had stepped out of the tub and wrapped my robe around her. She had tried on one of my dresses, but couldn't zip it.

'What are we going to do?' she asked.

141

I went to Zeke's chifforobe and brought Helen a pair of trousers and a short-sleeved shirt. 'You can wear these for now. I have to go down for lunch. Will you be okay up here by yourself?'

She nodded.

'Don't worry. I'll be right back. Do not open the door.' I left her and headed downstairs for yet another tray.

* * *

Mrs Griswold and Daphne were in the kitchen, along with Toby, who sat at a small table in the corner eating a sandwich with the crusts cut off, grape jelly smeared all over his face.

'Aunt Sarah, I'm having grape jelly,' he said.

'I can see that.' I smiled at Daphne and Mrs Griswold. 'Would you mind if I took a lunch tray up to my room? I'm so busy.'

Mrs Griswold opened a cupboard and took out an extra tray. 'What would you like?'

'Oh, don't trouble yourself, Mrs Griswold. I don't mind doing for myself. And I hope you don't mind that I came down for a snack earlier. I'll bring both trays back down, so you don't have to make an extra trip.'

'If only everyone was as good and kind as you two,' Mrs Griswold said to Daphne and me. She busied herself, slicing some bread for my tray. She gave me some cold chicken, a hardboiled egg, and two slices from a loaf of bread. 'You've got quite an appetite today. Are you eating for two? It would be so wonderful to have a baby in the house.'

'Sarah?' Daphne's voice was incredulous.

'I'm not pregnant,' I said. 'Just hungry. Honest.' I smiled at them as I carried the tray laden with food up to my room. I caught Daphne's reflection in the mirror. She watched me as I walked away from her, a strange expression on her face.

Helen held the door for me, as I carried the tray into the room. Zeke's pants were tight through the hips, big through the waist,

142

and much too long. Her wet hair hung in damp tendrils down her back. She eyed the tray.

'You must still be starved. I got as much food as I could without arousing suspicion. We can share.' We divvied up the chicken and the slices of bread and butter. I gave Helen the hardboiled egg. We sat in companionable silence, eating.

'She's very beautiful,' Helen said.

'Who?'

'Rachel.' She nodded at the portrait above the fireplace.

'Did you know her?'

'Not very well. She always had a kind word for everyone, no matter who you were. She was tough, I'll give her that. Arliss Winslow tried to be rude to her once, but Rachel made quick work of her. She didn't put on airs, if you know what I mean. Rachel knew who she was and where she came from. Marrying William didn't change her.' Helen's voice was sleepy again. 'I'm so tired. I'm afraid I need to sleep some more.'

'Why don't you lie back down? I have some work to finish. When Zeke gets back, we'll figure out what to do with you.'

'I'll speak to Joe Connor. But you have to promise to keep that Detective Bateson away from me.'

'Helen, what did you see?'

'I saw who put the rucksack in Simon's desk. I'll tell Joe and Wade Connor what I saw, but not until they bury their father. Will you keep me here until then?'

'Of course,' I said.

'You can't tell anyone I'm here.'

'Agreed.'

'What about Zeke? You can't speak for him.'

'I give you my word. If Zeke insists you go to Detective Bateson – which he won't, believe me – I'll help you leave. I'll give you money and sneak you out of the house.'

'You'd defy your husband?'

I ignored her question.

We were interrupted by a knock on the door. Helen dashed into the bathroom.

'Sarah, it's me. Why in the world have you locked the door?'

I opened the door for Zeke. He kicked off his shoes and sat down on the couch, leaned back and shut his eyes. I sat next to him, not quite sure how to broach the subject of Helen.

'What is it, my love?' he asked without looking at me.

'How did you know?'

'You've something to tell me. You're wound up tight as a drum, and you're about to burst with the news of it.' He opened his eyes and met my gaze. 'What is it?'

'Helen's here.'

'Here?'

'She ran out of her house when Detective Bateson showed up. It seems she got a ride part of the way and walked a good distance as well. She is utterly exhausted.'

'And?'

'And I promised we'd keep her safe until after Ken Connor's funeral. Then she'll speak to Joe and Wade. No one else.'

'You made a promise on my behalf?'

'No. I told her that if you didn't agree, I'd help her leave,' I said.

He kissed me, and for the briefest moment I forgot that Helen was hiding in the bathroom, listening to every word we said.

'She's in the bathroom,' I whispered into Zeke's ear.

'I don't care,' he whispered back, holding me tighter and kissing me again.

I laughed and pushed away from him.

'Helen, come out here,' Zeke said.

Helen came out of the bathroom and stood before Zeke, dressed in his clothes.

'She left without her clothes, and mine didn't fit,' I said.

'You don't want to speak to Detective Bateson?'

'No, sir. He won't believe a word I say.' She lifted her chin and

144

met Zeke's eyes. 'Mr Zeke, what I saw, it's going to ruin this family. You'll hate me.' She started to sob. 'And Simon – everyone will know how I feel ... I'm so ashamed.'

I went to Helen and put my arms around her. 'There, there.' I patted her back and soothed her as if she were an infant. I met Zeke's eyes.

'Helen, we'll keep you hidden until after the funeral. It's only for one night. After that, you must go to Joe. Agreed?'

Helen nodded, pushing away from me.

Zeke said, 'I'll arrange for some appropriate clothes to be delivered to the house. Write down your size for me. I'm going to change. I have to go back to work.'

'Yes, sir. Thank you, sir.' She went into the bathroom and shut the door behind her.

* * *

Once Helen had eaten her fill, exhaustion set in. Since Zeke would be staying at the mill through the night, I made a pallet on the floor in my room between the bed and wall. She curled up like a child and slept for eighteen hours, straight through. Toby snuck back down to the kitchen during the night and ate a whole jar of grape jelly, making himself sick in the process. Daphne had her hands full the next morning tending to him. Mrs Griswold left for the weekend to visit her son, which gave me free range to take up trays of food for Helen and myself. Around noon a delivery came from the local dress shop with a package of clothes for Helen. Zeke had arranged for two dresses, shoes, a hat, gloves, and stockings. At least Helen wouldn't have to go about in Zeke's clothes. We remained cloistered that entire next day, unable to do anything until Zeke made arrangements for Helen to speak to Joe Connor.

By 10 p.m., Zeke still hadn't come home. Helen and I prepared for bed, but Helen was growing restless, and I knew that if she didn't see Joe by tomorrow, she would in all likelihood leave us for good. She was a resourceful young woman, who could easily make her way to Los Angeles and start over with a new name. If she got away, we would never see her again.

We were lying in our respective beds, Helen on the floor next to me, when she spoke. 'You've seen Rachel, haven't you?'

I nearly lied. I almost opened my mouth and told Helen that of course I hadn't spoken to Rachel. After all, Rachel was dead and everyone knew that ghosts were nothing but figments of imagination, fanciful tales told on dark and stormy nights, designed to scare children. But I was asking Helen to trust me, and what better way to win trust than to give it?

'Yes,' I said. 'She came to me in Sausalito and told me if I found the emeralds, I would discover who killed her. When I found the emeralds in Simon's room, Rachel took me there.'

'Have you seen her since then?' Helen's voice wobbled with the promise of tears.

'No,' I said. 'She's been noticeably absent. She told me she'd give me a dream, but that hasn't happened either.'

'Do you think she knows who killed her?'

'I don't think so,' I said.

'Simon didn't kill Rachel.' Helen's voice rang with conviction.

'I know.' I turned on the bedside light and met Helen's eyes.

'When I tell Joe Connor what I know,' Helen said, 'this family is going to hate me, even you.'

'Not me, Helen,' I promised. 'And if you tell the truth, which I believe you will, not Zeke.'

'How can you know that?'

'Because there is never anything wrong with the truth. Now let's get a good night's sleep. Tomorrow is the funeral, and after that, you will speak to Joe and Wade.'

'Thank you, Miss Sarah,' Helen said. 'I wouldn't be here if it weren't for you.'

'Of course you would.' I turned off my bedside lamp and fell quickly to sleep.

146

Chapter 16

The day of Ken Connor's funeral dawned overcast and gray, perfect to suit my mood. As for Helen, Zeke had assured us that Wade and Joe would speak to her today, not at the police station, but at the mill. I would be glad to see Helen safely out of my hands. She had grown restless, and I was ready to have my small space in the house back to myself. We were working together to change the sheets and tidy the room when Daphne knocked once and barged in. Helen ran into the bathroom and closed the door behind her, just in the nick of time.

'Is someone in your bathroom?'

'No. The breeze shuts the door like that sometimes.' She carried a new vase of flowers in her arms, this one a simple crystal design with a band of gold around the rim. 'Another find at an antique store?'

'Estate sale, actually.' She set the vase on my dresser and fiddled with the stems until they were arranged to her satisfaction. Sunflowers this time, about two dozen of them. 'Do you like it?'

'Beautiful.' I picked up the robe that lay across the bed. 'I was just going to bathe.'

'Of course. Do you have linens? I can check—'

'No, I've got everything I need.' I got to the bathroom door before she did, and blocked it. 'Is everything okay?' She scrutinized me. 'You're acting funny, and you've got horrible circles under your eyes. Are you not sleeping well?' 'Not really. But I'll sleep well tonight, really.'

'Let me know if you need a sleep draught.' Daphne gave me a tight smile that didn't quite reach her eyes. 'I'm to drive us to the funeral. I'll see you downstairs at eleven-thirty, if that suits.'

'Yes, fine. Thanks.'

* * *

Ken Connor's intimate graveside service was short and somber. Lavinia Connor, Wade, and Joe sat on the only three chairs. Granna, Zeke, Simon, Daphne, and I, along with Sophie and Arliss, were the only people in attendance. When the casket was lowered, Lavinia went forward and tossed a red rose on top of it. When she broke down and wept, Wade and Joe led her to the waiting limousine.

Ken Conner served on the Millport Police for forty years. He was a loved and respected member of this tiny community, so it seemed the whole town showed up at the Connors' house for the reception after the service. The Connors lived in a mid-nine-teenth-century farmhouse, complete with a wrap-around porch and surrounded by rose bushes in full bloom. The interior of the house was comfortable, lived in, and, like Lavinia and Ken Connor, without pretense. A long trestle table had been covered with white linen and was rapidly filling with casseroles, fresh bread, pies, and vegetable dishes. A punch bowl with lemonade had been set up for the children, and white-coated waiters circled the room serving champagne and orange juice. By tacit agreement no one spoke of the murders. Thunder banged away in the distance. Conversation centered on the rain that would surely come in the afternoon, and the war.

I mingled, made small talk, nodded when a response was

expected. Soon Helen would go to the mill with Zeke and Wade. There she would tell her story – whatever it was – to the men who had promised to help her. Zeke, Joe, and Wade stood huddled by themselves in the corner, speaking in hushed voices. Every now and then Wade would scan the room, missing nothing. When his gaze lingered on his mother, I was surprised by the softness I saw there. I reached for another champagne and took my drink over to a sofa under the ceiling fan. I could have started a conversation with any number of people, but I didn't. I chose to sit by myself and people watch. I breathed a sigh of relief every time a newcomer would circulate away from me and onto a new group.

Sophie Winslow moved through the buffet, filling two plates with a little serving from each dish. She wore a linen suit, her bare legs tan and muscular. When she had gone through the buffet line, Joe broke away from Zeke and Wade, took one of the plates from Sophie, and followed her to the sofa. They sat close enough that their thighs touched. Across the room, Arliss Winslow watched them, cheeks hot, eyes ablaze. Sophie, oblivious to her mother's gaze, looked radiant, and didn't even flinch when Arliss approached her.

'Sophie, may I have a word, please? Joe, if you'll excuse us.' Arliss's voice cut through the hum of the party. Lavinia, Wade, and Zeke stood near the buffet. A hush fell over the room. Not a sound cut through the air.

'We're eating, Mother. Surely it can wait.'

'I'm afraid it can't,' Arliss said.

'I'll speak to you when I've finished eating, Mother,' Sophie said.

All eyes were riveted on Arliss Winslow and the unfolding scene. Wade and Zeke both wore a sardonic grin, as if they knew a secret.

'Young lady, you'll do as I say,' Arliss snapped.

'Mrs Winslow—' Joe tried to speak.

'Young man, stay out of this,' Arliss said.

'I will not,' Joe said. He stood up and stepped around the table. 'You won't speak to her that way.'

'Don't you condescend to me, Joe Connor. You may think because you lost an arm and came home a hero, you can speak to me like that. I will not have it.' Someone in the crowd gasped.

'We're engaged.' Sophie spoke in a calm, measured voice. She got up and stood near Joe. He put his arm around her. Lavinia came around to stand next to Sophie. *She's surrounded by love.* The thought sprung out of nowhere, but there it was. Sophie was with her new family. I knew it, just as I knew the sun would set in the evening.

'Engaged?' Arliss's eyes ravaged Joe, Sophie, and Lavinia. 'I suppose you knew about this, Lavinia?'

'I was very pleased at the news,' Lavinia said, her voice kind. She put an arm around Sophie. 'I've always wanted a daughter. I'm in need of companionship now that Ken is gone, and they will need a chaperone. Joe has his own apartment—'

'Do you think he can provide for her, give her the life to which she has become accustomed? He's a cripple.'

'That's enough, Mother. What life have I become accustomed to? You hovering over me, not letting me do anything, not letting me socialize with anyone because they aren't good enough? I'm tired of it. I'm getting married to Joe. I don't need your permission.'

'You are going to live on a policeman's salary?'

'Now see here,' Joe said.

'As long as you live under my roof,' Arliss said, 'you will do as you're told. I forbid this nonsense. Get your purse. We are leaving.'

'I'm not leaving,' Sophie said. 'I'm staying here.'

'You'll do no such thing,' Arliss said. Joe, Lavinia, and Sophie faced her, a united front. 'Fine. I forbid you to cross the threshold into my home. You can have the clothes on your back, and that is all.' She nodded at Joe. 'You want her? You can have her.' She put on her black gloves one at a time.

'So you're not too shocked when you get home,' Sophie said, 'I've taken my things. My clothes and my furniture. I had them moved out while you were at the hairdresser's this morning.'

'Your furniture?'

'Yes, mother. The pieces that grandmother left me. They are mine. I took them.' Everything happened so fast. Arliss lifted her hand to slap Sophie. Sophie was quicker. She grabbed Arliss's hand and moved close to her. 'Stop it, Mother. I'm done being bullied by you.'

'You can either give us your blessing or leave,' Joe said.

Arliss looked around the room. All eyes were upon her. All of her neighbors, the people to whom she had acted so superior, looked at her with pitying expressions. Her color drained away.

'Go to hell.' She looked around the room. 'All of you.' She turned and walked out of the house, slamming the door behind her.

One monumental collective sigh marked Arliss Winslow's departure. And just like that, the moment was over. Someone put a classical piano concerto on the phonograph. The waiters circled with fresh champagne. Soon conversation flowed. Arliss had taken the tension with her.

Zeke, who had come to stand behind me during the scene between Sophie and her mother, took my hand. Together we approached Joe, Lavinia, and Sophie.

'Are you okay?' Joe took a handkerchief out of his pocket and wiped his brow.

'I feel wonderful,' Sophie said. 'Now I wonder why I didn't do that years ago.'

'Never mind that, dear,' Lavinia said. 'Your mother will come around, just you wait and see. Meanwhile, you've got us. I'm so happy to welcome you to the family.'

'Mother, I'm going to propose a toast to the couple, if you don't mind.'

'Go ahead, dear,' Lavinia said.

151

'It's an unusual thing for a funeral, I know,' Wade said.

'And when have we ever been usual?' Lavinia smiled at her son.

Wade walked to the middle of the room. He picked up a spoon from the buffet and clanked it on his glass.

'Ladies and gentlemen,' he said. Everyone stopped and looked up at Wade. Those who were sitting in the other room came in. 'My dad was a great man who always put family first. Those of us who are here today are the people my father loved. You are our family. I'm sorry my dad isn't here to witness this event, but I am certain that he would approve. I would like to propose a toast to my brother and Sophie. Here's to your upcoming marriage. May your life together be filled with love, happiness, and – please god – grandchildren for my mother.' A murmur of laughter ran through the room. Wade held up his glass. 'To Joe and Sophie.'

'Joe and Sophie,' we said in unison.

Joe and Sophie held up their glasses while we drank to them. Soon everyone circled around the couple, wishing them congratulations. I followed Zeke, who shook Joe's hand and hugged Sophie.

'Congratulations,' I said to Joe.

'Thanks, Sarah.' He smiled at me.

'Best wishes, Sophie.' I waited for her to bite my head off. She gave me a shy smile – a gesture so out of character that I almost dropped my glass of champagne.

'Don't look so surprised, Sarah. I'm really not that mean. Maybe it's time we bury the hatchet,' Sophie said. 'I've been horrible to you. Forgive me?'

'Already done.' I wanted to tell Sophie that I knew who she was and what she had done. I understood her now. Secure in the knowledge that Wade Connor would deal with Sophie, I moved away from the crowd. 'I'm going to walk home,' I said to Zeke.

'By yourself?' Zeke said.

'Of course. Why not? You've got FBI people all over the place. What could go wrong?'

Wade Connor stood next to me. 'Zeke and I can take you. We're about to go get Helen. I'm going to meet with the county prosecutor after I speak with her.'

'I'd really rather walk, if you don't mind. I just want a little time to myself.'

'I don't like it,' Zeke said.

'There's been no sign of any of Hendrik Shrader's men,' Wade said. 'Do you have your gun?'

I opened my purse and showed them the gun.

'Where's Daphne or Granna? Get one of them to go with you,' Zeke said.

'I don't know where they are.'

'Just hurry,' Zeke said. 'It's going to rain and be mindful of lightning.'

'You won't leave Helen?'

'No,' Zeke said.

'See you at home.' I left Zeke and Wade and headed out into the overcast afternoon.

* * *

The sun broke through the clouds just as I reached Toby's swing. Someone – Daphne in all likelihood – had scattered sunflower seeds along the trail. They bloomed into abundant thatches of yellow along the path. I sat on the swing and took off my stockings, tucking them into my purse. At one point I thought I heard footsteps on the path behind me. Bushes rustled. Birds stopped singing. I reached into my purse, grateful that I was armed, and waited. Soon the birds started chirping. I chastised myself for letting Helen's anxiety rub off on me. Something didn't feel right.

'Hello? Who's there?' I called out. No one answered.

Lightning cracked through the sky like an arrow from heaven.

I counted to three before the thunder bumped, remembering the five-seconds-equals-a-mile credo. I ran toward the abandoned barn where Zeke and I had our picnic, not caring if anyone followed me. Another bolt of lightning shot from the sky, and this time the thunder was right on its heels. The air around the barn smelled of electricity. Without thinking, I opened the old door, desperate for a safe place. When I looked back at this later, I would realize that the rusty hinges should have squeaked, but they didn't. Someone had oiled the door. I propped it open for the light and hoped that when the rain did come, the metal roof would prove sound.

I ignored the smell of mouldy hay and fuel and moved deeper into the building, looking for a place to sit. A rusty tractor lay under decades of dust. Outside the thunder and lightning raged. A shiver ran down my spine; goose bumps covered my arms and the back of my neck. I stopped, stood in the middle of the barn, listening for footsteps, the sound of someone else's breath, certain in the knowledge that I was being watched.

'Hello?' I called out. My heart pounded in my chest.

The barn door swung shut, leaving me in darkness. The bolt clicked home, locking me in.

Footsteps moved outside. I ran to the door, pushed on it, but the old wood held fast.

'Help!' I shouted and pounded on the door, to no avail. Was there a window in here? After a few seconds my eyes adjusted to the light, and I saw an old ladder, which led to the hayloft above.

'Let me out, please.' I beat the door with my fist.

No one answered. Someone stood outside the barn. The sound of ripping newspaper puzzled me at first, but when the paper was stuffed under the locked door by a gloved hand and gasoline – for there was no mistaking the smell – was poured on the rumpled paper, the gravity of my situation sunk in.

In the dim light I could just make out the tiny rivulets of liquid that flowed under the dried wood of the walls, carving rivers in the dirt. Outside, my assailant didn't speak, but his breath came in short, rapid bursts. Every sound was magnified. I heard the head of the match as it brushed on the box. He threw the match down, and with a whoosh the rivers turned into liquid flames. They spread along the front of the dry building in an instant. When the fire reached the stack of hay, the flames consumed it, and grew. Desperate, I looked around the room, my eyes tearing from the smoke that burned my lungs. The ladder.

I ran toward it, holding my breath. Tears ran down my cheeks. Behind me, the flames grew larger. I grabbed onto the bottom rung, ignoring the huge splinter that wedged into the pad of my thumb. Praying that the rotten wood would support my body weight, I hoisted myself up the ladder and onto the weak floorboards in the hayloft. Soon the floor beneath me would catch fire. Before me, the opening loomed. I would need to jump. A broken bone was better than being burned alive. Just as I got close, the flames crept up through the wood floor. I heard voices.

'Sarah?' Zeke stood outside.

I ran to the opening and saw Zeke looking up at me.

'What do I do?'

'Jump. You have to jump,' Zeke said.

Soon Wade came running out of the shrubs. I heard Wade say, 'How in the hell did this fire start?' He carried a gray army blanket. He unfolded it. They held it taut between them.

'Jump onto the blanket. It will break the fall,' Zeke said. 'Sarah, the building is going to collapse. You have to jump. We have to move away from the building before it collapses. Jump!'

I closed my eyes and jumped.

Chapter 17

The blanket did little to break the fall. When I hit the ground, my breath left my body, as though sucked out by a vacuum. Zeke and Wade pulled me to my feet and dragged me away from the building while I struggled for breath.

We had just gotten clear of the smoke and heat when the old barn collapsed in a burning heap of flames. The embers flew toward the sky and scattered on the ground. We all stood by, watching as the grass in front of the barn caught fire. When the wind picked up, the fire spread over the dry golden grass.

'We need to get some help,' Zeke said. 'It's dry as tinder around here.'

'Let's get to the car. It's just at the road. We'll have to hurry and call the fire department.'

'Can you walk?' Zeke said.

'Yes.' I wasn't in any pain. In fact, I really couldn't feel anything. 'I'm fine.' I took a wobbly step.

'She's not fine,' Wade said.

'Lean on me.' Zeke put his arm around me. No one spoke as we walked toward the road, away from the crackling flames. The sky grew darker by the minute. Just as we approached Wade's car, the clouds opened and the rain fell. I tipped my face up toward

156

it, not caring that I would be dragged home looking like a wet dog.

Wade got behind the wheel. Zeke scooted into the back with me. My teeth had started to chatter. Zeke wrapped the blanket around me.

'She's in shock,' Zeke said.

'I'm driving as fast as I can,' Wade snapped. 'I can't see.'

'What happened back there, Sarah?' Zeke asked.

'Someone locked me in the barn,' I said.

'Did you see who did it?' Wade asked.

'No,' I whispered. My throat was utterly parched. I would have given anything for a glass of water.

'What were you doing on the path?' I asked. I felt warm and loopy, as though someone had given me an injection of opium.

'Wade's car was blocked in, so I was going to get our car and pick him up,' Zeke said.

'And then the Belmonts left, so I was able to move my car. I was driving looking for Zeke when I saw the smoke and pulled over.' Wade watched me through the rear-view mirror.

'What made you grab a blanket?' Zeke asked.

'I don't know,' Wade said. 'I always carry one in my trunk.'

I tried to speak, but the effort of it hurt my throat. Zeke's face started undulating in slow rolling waves. His voice faded away, even though his lips moved. I felt myself lose consciousness as I went down, down, down.

'It was Rachel,' I said, my voice scratchy. And everything went black.

* * *

When I awoke, Zeke sat next to my bed. His damp hair hung over his collar. The smell of gasoline brought everything back to me. I sat up.

'I need to wash.' My words came out as a dry bark.

157

'Good morning, my love,' Zeke said. He helped me to sit up and propped pillows behind me. He poured a tall glass of ice water out of the pitcher next to the bed. I gulped it greedily, savoring the feel of the cold liquid as it soothed my throat.

'What time is it?' My stomach rumbled.

Zeke poured me some beef tea out of a thermos that sat on the table. 'Drink this. You've been asleep for almost fourteen hours.' I sipped the warm broth. Nothing had ever tasted so good.

'The doctor's examined you. He gave you a shot to let you rest,' Zeke said. 'You remember what happened?'

'The fire,' I said. 'Is Helen okay? What happened?'

Zeke met my eyes, but he didn't speak. 'Can we leave that for now? Why don't you take a bath? While you're doing that, I'll put some sheets on the bed that don't stink of smoke and fuel, and get Mrs Griswold to bring you up a tray. After you've eaten, I'll tell you everything.'

'Zeke—'

'You need to care for yourself right now, Sarah. I'll tell you everything, but first things first.'

Half an hour later, I sat on the sofa, the slightest smell of smoke and gasoline lingering in my hair, an empty plate in front of me. I had eaten two eggs and an entire bowl of chicken and vegetable soup, despite my sore throat, which, according to Zeke, would get better in a day or two.

'Now tell me,' I said. 'Who did Helen see? Have the police made any arrests?'

'Daphne,' Zeke said.

'What?'

'No one is quite sure what to believe,' Zeke said. 'Detective Bateson all but spat in her face. Simon is shocked. He believes Helen, of course, but it's hard to rationalize that his wife is a cold-blooded murderer.'

'But why in the world would Daphne murder Rachel and Ken Connor?'

158

'That we don't know. But Helen swears she saw Daphne come into the room carrying the rucksack. Helen saw her open it and put the emeralds in the bag. Detective Bateson grilled her about it, so did Joe, and so did Wade. She never changed her story, not once. She didn't flinch. She was utterly credible. I believe her.'

'And Daphne? Where is she?'

'Gone,' Zeke said.

'Gone?'

'There's a nationwide manhunt for the woman. We'll find her.' Zeke stood up. He walked to the window, his limp more pronounced today than it had been for a while. He moved the curtains aside and stared out at the pasture. 'She saw Helen as we were taking her down to the mill. I thought Helen was going to throw up when she ran into Daphne. If I had been paying attention, I would have picked up on that. Daphne, being smarter than the average person, knew in an instant what Helen was about. After Helen told us what she saw, Joe came to get Daphne to take her in for questioning. She was gone. She had taken a small bag with her, but she was gone.

'Is there any proof? What about the emeralds?'

Zeke shook his head. 'It's going to be Helen's word against Daphne's word, I'm afraid. If Daphne has the emeralds, she's taken them with her. We've nothing to go on. We've no proof that she took the emeralds, no proof that she ever had the emeralds.

'Zeke, I'm so sorry,' I said. 'How's Helen?'

'She's holding up,' Zeke said. 'Frightfully strong girl. She's at her father's. Simon has been with her.'

'Does Simon believe her?'

'Yes, he does.' He bent down and kissed me on the forehead. 'He's distraught and relieved, if you can believe that. He and Daphne haven't been husband and wife for some time now. She tried to kill you, too, Sarah. We found a fuel can and stacks of newspaper in the backseat of her car.'

159

'My god,' I said. 'Do you think she'll come back? What are we supposed to do?'

'Nothing,' Zeke said. 'We're going to let the authorities do their job. They'll find her. She left in a hurry, didn't take her purse or anything, only the clothes on her back. It's possible she's hidden the emeralds around the house and will come back for them.'

'And then she'll go to trial. I cannot even imagine the media circus that will entail. I'm surprised Nick Newland isn't here already.'

'Wade's taken care of Nick Newland. And as for the press, they haven't got wind of anything. There's hope that Daphne will be captured before the week lets out. Let's just wait and see what happens.' He kissed me. 'I need to make a few phone calls. I'll be back shortly. Will you be alright by yourself?'

'Yes,' I said.

'Good. You're to stay in bed today, doctor's orders.'

'Fine. But tomorrow I'm going to see Helen.'

'Fine,' Zeke said.

Wade and Zeke were worried enough to keep a man outside my door. I got up, padded over to the door and double checked the lock. My throat felt dry again, as if there weren't enough water in the world to quench my endless thirst. Daphne's vase of flowers sat on my desk. Zeke had left the Final Morning Edition of the *San Francisco Chronicle* on the coffee table. 'COAL STRIKE IS ON! BUT MINERS OFFER TO WORK FOR U.S.!' Sixty-four thousand miners walked off the job. Soon the country wouldn't have any electricity. I could not have cared less.

I opened the French doors and took the clean air in through my nose, since sucking oxygen in through my mouth burned the back of my throat. The rain had mitigated the heat and washed the dust away. Outside, the greenery was clean and crisp, and the smell of damp earth and sweet grass lifted my spirits. Thoughts of Daphne, Simon, Ken Connor, and poor, poor Toby ran through my mind. What would become of that child when he discovered what his mother had done? At least Simon was exonerated. At least Toby and Simon would have each other. Meanwhile, Daphne remained on the loose, and there was no physical proof whatsoever that she had the emeralds or that she had committed the murders. I longed to do something productive, something that would move Zeke's and my life forward, but it seemed as though we were in a perpetual state of limbo, at least until Daphne was caught. And for the time being anyway, that is where we would stay. I ran this pattern of thoughts through my head over and over and over.

Stop it! I chastised myself. I needed to do something, and when my eyes lit on a fresh bunch of pages from Dr Geisler, I decided to work. I fixed my hair and dressed. I was sitting on the sofa pulling up my stockings when the sunlight caught Daphne's vase of flowers. The effect dazzled. The light reflected off the crystal facets and threw glints onto the wall. The green orbs in the bottom of the vase shimmered with a life force all their own. I stared, not quite ready to believe what I saw.

Without thinking, I picked up the vase, tossed the flowers on the table, and carried it into the bathroom. I dumped the water down the sink and pulled the marbles that had come from Toby's toy box out of the bottom of the vase. I wrapped them in a towel and carried them into the living area where I opened the towel and spread them out on top of it. There, among the cats eyes and spearmint swirls, were the emeralds, hidden right in front of our noses this whole time.

I opened the door and called out to the policeman in the hallway. He had placed a chair outside my door and had just fallen asleep. I didn't blame him. I coughed.

I coughed again.

He jumped up, almost falling over his own feet in the process. 'Would you please go get Zeke?' I asked.

'I'm sorry. I was told not to leave you.'

'It's important. Go get him. Now.' I used my bossy voice and slammed the door for emphasis, confident that the young man would do my bidding. Sure enough, I heard footsteps as he headed down the stairs.

I unwrapped the emeralds and set them out on the towel in the sunlight. There were sixteen of them all told. Each and every single one of them stunning in its own right.

'I see you've found my little secret.' Daphne's voice startled me. Behind her, the French doors were open wide. She still wore the dress that she had on at Ken's funeral, but two days of wear had made it dull and dirty. It reeked of gasoline, a remnant of her attempt to burn me alive. Her hair was loose around her shoulders, but it was dingy from not being washed.

'I don't know what you're talking about.' I swept the emeralds into my pocket.

'I had to kill her,' Daphne said. 'Rachel. I had to do it. For Toby. You understand, I'm sure. Sit here.' She patted the empty spot next to her on the sofa. I sat down. The smell of her should have made me gag, but fear overtook me. She devoured the toast that lay on the tray before she poured out coffee in the mug I had used earlier, not minding that my lipstick stained the rim.

'We probably don't have much time, but I want to tell you, want to explain myself.'

'You don't have to tell me anything—'

She kept on talking, as though I weren't there.

'Simon burned through the trust my mother set up for me. He gambled it away. Of course, when a woman marries, her property becomes her husband's, at least that's what my mother believed. I should have killed her, too. I needed my own money, and I refused to be in the position where I had to beg for funds from anyone, but especially from an idiot like Simon. I only married him to get away from my mother. We never told anyone that Simon had such horrible gambling debts. Will Sr would have kicked us out of the house, and Toby would have no inheritance.'

Daphne crossed her legs. 'I couldn't let Rachel get pregnant,

162

couldn't let her have a child. That would have ruined everything for Toby. We were friends, you know. We used to take coffee every morning, so I gave her pennyroyal, slipped it into her drink when she wasn't looking. I had to protect Toby. If Rachel got pregnant, Toby would have been out of the picture for good. There wouldn't have been any hope of my son inheriting a penny, never mind the property, the mill, and the prestige of being the heir. You'd think the little bitch would have stopped trying.' Daphne clasped her hands on her lap, her action prim, proper, and incongruous to this gruesome revelation. 'Then one day she wanted to borrow something and went into my dresser. She found the pennyroyal. She recognized it right away and realized what I had done. It's an abortifacient. Do you know what that is? It prevents the embryo from clinging to the uterine wall, resulting in a miscarriage.'

A shadow moved on the balcony behind us, as the policeman sidled up to the open French door. Zeke was with him, and I realized they must have accessed the porch from Granna's room.

'So I had to kill her. I stayed home with Toby that Christmas Eve while everyone went to Mother's party. Rachel was pregnant – she hadn't announced it yet, but I knew. A mother can tell these things. I thought she'd tire of the party and come home early, and I knew she'd take the path by the lake. All I had to do was give Toby a tiny bit of valerian in his milk. He was a good baby, my Toby was. He went fast asleep. After he was sleeping soundly, I bundled up in my warm clothes, went out to the path by the lake, and hid in the bushes. My timing was perfect. When Rachel walked by, I pushed her and knocked her off balance. She landed in the shallow water on her hands and knees. She had on a fur coat and a long dress, which weighed her down. It wasn't difficult for me to push her down. I sat on her back, pinning her flailing arms with my legs, as I held her face under water. I did it for Toby, and I almost got away with it.

'But Ken Connor – my god, that man just wouldn't give up. He worked that case to the point of obsession. I had been very careful and knew that as long as I didn't have to sell the emeralds, Ken would never catch me. I knew he wouldn't live forever and once he was gone, I could go to New York or Paris and get rid of the stones discreetly.'

I sat, mute and numb, in the face of my sister-in-law.

'But then Simon's gambling got out of hand. He owed a lot of money and there was no way to pay them. I could not expose Toby to that. My stupid husband was my undoing. I had to sell some of the stones. Simon has never won at gambling. He's too much of an idiot. I sold one stone a year ago, after vetting the buyer's, making sure they would cut into smaller pieces. Once it was cut, I would be safe. Alas, men are greedy. This particular gentleman sold the emerald intact, and bragged while he did it. After that, it was only a matter of time before the stone was traced to me. When Ken Connor found the jeweler he had to go, and I had to kill him before he told everyone that he had located the man to whom I had sold the emeralds.

'And in case you are wondering, I pushed you that first night. I wanted you scared. You would have to go too, eventually, but I wasn't in any hurry.'

'Why?' I asked.

'Because your children will trump Toby,' Daphne spat the words, as though I were too stupid to comprehend.

I caught a glimpse of Zeke just then, standing on the balcony white-faced, his hands clenched into fists. The policeman stood next to him, his hand on his gun. Daphne babbled on, unaware that she had witnesses to her confession.

'Ken knew that I had killed Rachel. Don't look at me that way. I'm not a common criminal. You don't understand, Sarah. You've never had a child. One day you will understand. I did all of this for Toby. I'm sorry that I can't make you see that now. And I'm sorry, because I think you and I would have been friends.'

'But even if you kill everyone, Toby won't inherit.'

'Ah, you're not seeing the end result. I would have married

164

Zeke, after your tragic demise. And, believe me, he would have run into my arms. If Helen hadn't been in Simon's room when I planted the emeralds, my plan would have worked perfectly. Fast forward a year, maybe two, to your tragic death. Zeke and I would marry. I wouldn't have another child. A woman can control that. Toby would have been the only one, and everything would come to him.'

Daphne stood up and moved to the chair where I had set my purse. In an instant she had my gun in her hand.

'Daphne—'

'Shut up, Sarah. Just shut up.' She called out to Zeke. 'You two can come in now. I know you've been there listening to my sad tale.'

Zeke stepped into the room, fury in his eyes. His voice when he spoke was calm and measured. 'Why didn't you come to me, Daph? You know I would have helped you and provided for Toby.'

'Because I don't want charity from you or from anyone.' She pointed the gun at herself. 'Promise you'll take care of Toby.'

'Daphne,' Zeke said, his voice soft and soothing.

'Promise me!' she screamed.

'Of course, I'll take care of Toby,' Zeke said. 'I give you my word that I will treat him as though he is my own. He'll never want for anything. Now put down that damn gun and talk to me.'

She fired.

165

Chapter 18

The shot deafened me. Zeke and the policeman shouted at each other. Their mouths moved, but all I heard was a relentless ringing in my ears. Daphne remained on her feet, doubled over, clutching her stomach. I expected puddles of blood, but didn't see any. Not yet.

The two men hurried over to Daphne, each standing on one side. They balanced on bent knees, trying to get Daphne down on the floor. She hung between them, limp as a ragdoll. I thought for sure she was dead, but she tricked us. Out of the blue, she came to life, rose to her feet, and pushed Zeke and the agent hard. Zeke fell backwards, crashing into the coffee table. The policeman stumbled, almost fell, but was able to correct himself. By the time he stood up, Daphne had run out the French doors, climbed over the balcony, and shimmied down the post to the lawn below.

My hearing came back. The voices pierced the ringing.

'She's running toward the woods,' Zeke said

'She didn't even shoot herself,' Agent Wheeler said. The bullet had lodged itself into a floorboard, splintering it beyond repair in the process. He picked up the casing from the bullet and tucked it in his pocket, then climbed out the window and took off after Daphne.

'Are you able to stand?' I held out my hand to Zeke.

He took it and rose to his feet.

'Call Wade. Tell him what's happened.' He hurried out of the house to join in the hunt. His injured leg wouldn't let him climb out the window. I watched for a moment as Zeke tried to run in the same direction as Agent Wheeler and Daphne. Soon he slowed, his limp pronounced.

Thank goodness Wade happened to be at his mother's house. He answered the phone on the first ring. I didn't mince words. I told him what happened as succinctly as I could.

'On my way,' he said.

I had just placed the phone into the cradle when Granna and Toby came downstairs.

'We thought we heard a shot,' Granna said.

I eyed Toby.

'Really? I didn't hear anything. Maybe a car backfired.' I tousled Toby's hair and gave him a smile.

'Toby, go on upstairs. I'll bring you some ice cream,' Granna said.

'But it's only morning,' Toby said.

'I won't tell if you won't,' Granna said. 'Give me fifteen minutes.'

'Yes, ma'am,' Toby said. He flew up the stairs.

'I know a gunshot when I hear one. What's happened?'

'Daphne. She killed Rachel. She killed Ken Connor. She escaped out my bedroom window. Zeke and Agent Wheeler have gone after her.'

Granna pulled the flask from her pocket, took a swig and handed it to me. I started to shake my head and utter a polite *no, thank you*, but thought better of it. The brandy burned my throat and warmed my belly.

'Mrs Griswold is off today,' Granna said. 'I'll take Toby to her. She has a nice place in the country with a garden, goats, and plenty of things to keep the child busy.'

* * *

Detective Bateson came in his own car. Wade followed, with Simon and Helen in tow.

Helen's face was pale, but her eyes sparkled, despite the dark circles underneath them.

'Simon, I'm so sorry,' I said. We moved as a group into Will's study. Wade pushed everything that rested on the desk aside and spread out a map of the Caen property and the surrounding area.

'I'm not,' he said. 'Daphne and I have been living a charade since Toby came along. She didn't love me. She loved this.' He gestured to the house. 'She only married me to get away from her mother.'

'Simon,' Helen started to speak.

'Let's not talk about it now,' Simon said. He took Helen's hand as they sat next to each other on the sofa.

Wade continued to study the map, tracing potential routes with his fingers, while Detective Bateson stood by, his hands crossed over his chest.

'We'll find her,' Detective Bateson said. 'She's a woman. How far do you think she can get?'

Wade ignored him, picked up the phone, and dialed.

'This is what I want to do,' he said. He ordered men stationed at all the bus and train stations within one-hundred miles. He ordered that Daphne's bank be notified, and that they call immediately should she or anyone affiliated with her request money from her bank accounts. He gave a litany of instructions, casting a net so wide and tight that it was only a matter of time before Daphne became caught in it. Now all we had to do was sit and wait.

When Zeke came limping through the front door, I resisted the urge to run to him. Sophie was with him, her face pale and drawn.

'Joe's out with the search party, and I couldn't stay in that house any longer. I hope it's okay that I came here,' she said.

'Of course.'

168

She followed me into the study and said hello to everyone. Her eyes lit on Simon and Helen, sitting close and holding hands. Their closeness had no effect on her. She took the chair next to the couch.

'Simon, I am so sorry for the way my sister treated you. I hope that you and I can still—' Sophie buried her head in her hands and burst into tears.

We let her cry. Simon put a comforting hand on her back and handed her a handkerchief at the appropriate time.

'This isn't your fault, Soph. It's not anyone's fault. It's a ridiculous series of circumstances, and I'm glad that it's over.'

'But Daphne—' Sophie started to speak.

'Daphne is a murderer. I'm sorry, Sophie, but there you have it. She acts as though she has high ideals and does everything for Toby. Nonsense. She's greedy. I'm glad to be rid of her.' He stood up now and faced all of us. 'I'm going to be filing for divorce. I should have done so a long time ago.'

Zeke stood and went to his brother. Soon they were hugging.

'I've been such a fool,' Simon said.

Wade Connor had slipped out of the room and had missed Simon's revelation. He stood in the doorjamb of the study now, with Nick Newland standing next to him.

'What are you doing here?' I snapped.

'Hello, Sarah,' Nick said, as he stepped into the room.

'Sarah, Zeke, a word, please.' Wade said. 'Nick, the coffee is in the pot over there. Help yourself. I'll find you a place to work.'

The three of us stepped out into the hallway. Wade shut the door behind us.

Before I had a chance to speak, Zeke said, 'Just listen to what he has to say before you react.'

'I gave him the exclusive on Daphne. He wanted to write a story about you, Sarah. I had to bribe him. You two need to give him an interview. Don't look at me like that. It was part of the deal.'

'It's the best way,' Zeke said.

So we gave Nick Newland an interview. To his credit, he asked solid questions and had done his homework. He knew of Ken Connor's passion for Rachel Caen's case. He expressed appropriate respect for the man's death. Wade stayed with me, and the time flew by. Two hours later, Zeke came in to rescue me.

'That's enough, Newland. We've had a rough time of it, and Sarah could use a break,' Zeke said.

'Of course.' He stood, shook hands with Zeke and me.

* * *

It seemed like hours until everyone left. Simon took Sophie home. He decided to let Toby stay with Mrs Griswold, at least for the next day or two. Wade, Zeke, and I were in our sitting room, sipping hot black coffee from the big mugs that the kitchen staff used. Outside, the rain pounded. We had lost electricity long ago and were sitting in the light cast by the candelabra. The events of the day washed over me, the surprise ending to a twisted story. I was numb to it now. Maybe the numbness let me see the solution to our other problem.

'I know how we can trap Sophie,' I said, 'and we can do it tomorrow night.'

* * *

'If she doesn't come in fifteen minutes, I am leaving,' Wade Connor said.

It had taken a lot of cajoling to convince Wade and Zeke that my plan would work. Earlier in the evening, while Joe, Helen, Simon, Sophie, Wade, Zeke, and I were having dinner – cold sandwiches and hot coffee prepared by Granna, who insisted that we eat even though no one wanted to – we simply hinted that we had indeed found the emeralds and had hidden

170

them in the hollowed poster of Daphne's bed. 'The Climber will never find them. They'll be safe until we can figure out what to do with them. In all likelihood we will need to sell them to pay back the insurance company for the claim they paid out, or just give them to the insurance company,' Zeke said.

'Good riddance to them,' Simon said. 'Those blasted stones have caused this family enough grief to last a lifetime.'

That is how Zeke, Wade, and I had wound up in Daphne's deserted room at two-thirty in the morning.

'She'll come. Just be patient,' I said. Zeke and I were sitting on the floor near the bathroom door, while Wade had positioned himself next to the armoire. We had been sitting in the dark, hiding, since ten-thirty.

'That's it,' Wade said. 'This is—'

There was no mistaking the sound of someone shimmying the copper pipe outside Daphne's window. Wade Connor stuck his nose in the air, as though sniffing out his prey. He waved at us and stepped out of sight. Zeke and I slipped into the bathroom. In a matter of seconds, the window opened. Footsteps light as air moved on the floor.

'Looking for these?' Zeke and I stepped out of the bathroom, just as Wade held up the bag of fake emeralds.

Sophie stood stock still. She was dressed head to toe in black, her face covered with a ski mask.

'Sophie, we know it's you,' Wade said. 'Take off the mask.' She moved toward the window. Zeke blocked her way.

'We want to help you,' Zeke said.

'By arresting me? By sending me to jail?' She tore the mask from her face and crumpled onto the floor.

'You little fool,' Wade said. 'Come on, get up. I know how to fix this.' He stood above her, holding out his hand.

'Fix it? You mean you are not going to send me to jail?' Her voice broke.

'I am going to save you one time. You get into trouble like this again, and you are on your own.'

'I don't know why I do it. I'm so ashamed. Joe ...' She took Wade's hand and let him help her to her feet.

'You're going to tell Joe everything. Daphne found out about you, didn't she? She knew you were stealing,' Wade said. 'He's going to be your husband, so you'd best not have any secrets.'

'She toyed with me,' Sophie said. 'She knew it was me, and somehow she always managed to find the things I had stolen. She would take my stash and put it back.' Sophie turned to me, 'That day in the woods, Sarah, I knew you were there. I had a feeling you would leave things where you had found them, knowing that Zeke and Joe would need to see them in their hiding place. So I waited in the bushes, and when you hurried away, I took the rucksack and hid it somewhere else.' She wiped her eyes. 'God, I'm glad this is over.' She gave Wade a beseeching look. 'I'm so exhausted.'

Wade put a protective arm around the girl and led her out the bedroom. We followed them down to the front door. When they had gone, we locked the door behind them and headed back upstairs, arm in arm.

'Now I know why Sophie looked so stricken when she came into the study and saw her rucksack. Daphne had stolen from her,' I said.

'She's lucky Daphne didn't set her up to take the fall for the murders she committed,' Zeke said.

'What's Wade going to do?' I asked.

'He didn't tell me, and I didn't ask.' He kissed my forehead. 'Let's get some sleep.'

Chapter 19

We slept until nine-thirty, when Helen knocked on the door before entering with a tray laden with coffee, toast, homemade jam, and scrambled eggs.

'It's good to have you back, Helen,' Zeke called to her from the bedroom.

I tied the belt of my robe as I went to the sitting room.

'Look at the newspaper.' She handed me the morning edition of the *Millport News*. The usual war headlines, 'YANKS IN 2000-MILE RAID ON JAP SHIPPING!' screamed across the top. Under that, in small letters, 'MILLPORT CLIMBER RETURNS LOOT.'

'*In an unprecedented act, the notorious cat burglar, who has successfully eluded the Millport Police Department for the past eight months, returned all of the stolen items. Imagine the surprise when Detective Bateson went to work this morning and found all the stolen items sitting on his desk.*

'*When asked if the police will continue to search for the Millport Climber, so the citizens of this town can know the identity of the man who committed these daring acts of thievery, Detective Bateson refused to comment ...*'

'It's hard to believe, isn't it?' Helen said. 'I imagine Wade Connor—'

'Best leave the questions unasked, Helen,' I said.

I knew that if I continued to read the paper, I would find stories about Daphne and how she continued to elude the police. She had been sighted in San Francisco, Portland, Seattle, and someone even said that she had stolen a plane and flown away. But I didn't look for those stories. I didn't want to read about Daphne. I spent my days – and a fair share of sleepless nights – trying to forget about her.

After Helen left us, Zeke and I sat at the small table, empty breakfast dishes surrounding us. A smile played on my husband's lips.

'What is it?'

He came over and kissed the back of my neck before he pulled his chair close to me and sat down. 'Are you happy here?'

'Yes,' I said. 'I'll never get used to this heat, but I've actually started to grow quite fond of this sleepy little town.'

'So you're okay with us staying on for a few more months? I really do need to see Simon settled. And there's a house in town, three bedrooms, lots of shade. I thought we could go and look at it this evening, if you've a mind to.'

I subscribe to the theory that all women need their own kitchens, and their own homes.

'When can we move in?' I asked.

'Let's look at it first, my love,' Zeke said, 'just to make sure we like it.'

* * *

We set out just as the sun went down, letting the full moon light our path.

'The June full moon is called the strawberry moon,' Zeke said. 'It serves as a signal that the fruit is growing ripe and will soon be ready for harvest.'

'Are you a witch?' I teased.

174

'Witches are women. Everyone knows that.' He grabbed my hand, turned it over and kissed my wrist. Shivers ran up my spine. Zeke chuckled.

'Let's not get distracted,' I said, breaking away from him.

The house was on a quiet cul-de-sac, two blocks off Main Street. The owner had left the front door unlocked for us, but the electricity had been turned off so we couldn't get a good look at it. The floors were of wide planked wood, polished to a shine, and there were lots of windows.

The fenced-in yard had a raised bed, ready for a small garden. I loved it at first sight.

'So I'll call Mrs Glensmith and tell her we'll take it,' Zeke said.

We were on our way back home, full of ideas and plans. We would have to buy quite a lot of new furniture, but we didn't care. We had lost everything. We would rebuild our lives, together. We came to the end of the woods, to the place where the trees gave way to the sloping lawn that led to the house. We stopped for a moment, basking in the moonlight. Zeke pulled me to him, and had just lowered his lips to mine, when I saw a light in our bedroom.

'Look.' I pointed to our bedroom window, where a light flickered. 'Someone's in our room.'

I broke away from Zeke and sprinted toward the house with all my might, ignoring my burning lungs. I bolted through the front door, up the stairs, and into the darkness. I tried the switch, but the light didn't work. It took a second for my eyes to adjust. The window, which I had closed before we left, gaped open now, the curtains pushed to the side. Someone had climbed out the window. Daphne?

'What happened?' Zeke came in behind me. We stood side by side, panting from exertion. Together we leaned out the window and watched, helpless, as Sophie landed on the gravel below and took off in a run down the sloping lawn, toward the trees.

'That was Sophie,' Zeke said. 'I can tell by the way she runs.'

175

He closed the window and pulled the curtains to. He tried the switch. The light worked this time. On my desk lay the box that held my pearls and the fountain pen that Zeke had given me. A small note, typewritten, sat on top of the box. '*I'm sorry.*'

'I would say that's a peace offering,' Zeke said.

Chapter 20

Days went by, and still Daphne managed to outsmart the police. Given the personal nature of the situation, a new FBI agent had been assigned to lead the manhunt. He held a press conference, vowed he would find her, dead or alive, and that was the last we heard from him.

We settled into a routine. Simon and Zeke worked long hours at the mill. Granna and Helen took care of Toby, and, in turn, took care of us. We started taking the evening meal together, with Mrs Griswold sitting at the table with us. In an effort to keep things simple, Simon and Helen told Toby that his mother had gone on a trip. We all went out of our way to keep Toby away from people who would tell him otherwise.

Despite all that had happened, we settled into a peaceful day-to-day existence.

One afternoon, I went downstairs for a piece of toast. The heat made me nauseated, and I often woke up feeling woozy, only to feel better after a light breakfast. The phone rang in the hall. I answered it.

'Sarah, do me a favor, please. Get Toby and Granna, and come to the stable. Can you be there in half an hour?' Simon didn't wait for me to answer. 'Excellent. See you then.' He hung up.

The three of us were waiting when Simon and Zeke drove up in the car. A truck followed them, pulling a horse trailer.

'What's in the trailer?' Granna asked.

'It's either empty or a small horse,' Toby said.

Granna, Helen, and I looked at each other, all of us realizing at the same time what Simon had done. Simon and Zeke got out of the car. Zeke came toward us, smiling, while Simon went to speak to the driver of the truck. Soon the man got out and walked around the back. He opened the trailer door. We all watched as a small pony, black as ink, backed out of the trailer.

'May I go to my dad?' Toby asked.

'Yes, child,' Granna said.

Rachel's ghost appeared next to Toby just as he took off running. She put a shimmery hand on his shoulder, and he checked himself, stopped running, and slowed to a walk as he neared the trailer. He approached the pony, but detoured to his father, where he put his arms around his leg and started to cry.

'What's the matter, old man?' Simon asked, as he swept Toby into his arms.

'I'm so happy, Daddy. Thank you.' He kissed his father's cheek before he wriggled free. He looked up at Rachel, who stood near him. No one seemed to notice what he was doing. She nodded and walked with him up to the pony. Rachel put her ghost hand out and the pony nuzzled it. She stepped away and nodded to Toby. While the cowboy held its lead, the child circled the patient animal, his actions a painful mimic of his mother. He ran his hands up and down the pony's legs and all over its body. For his part, the pony stood still, like a docile lamb. Once Toby was sure the pony was sound, he threw his arms around its neck.

'I'm going to call you Midnight,' he said.

'I've got to get back to work,' Simon said. 'But I'll be home for dinner.'

'Come on, Toby,' Helen said. She walked toward the boy. 'We'll help you get Midnight settled in the stable.' Toby had Midnight's lead, and with Helen walking next to him and Rachel's ghost trailing behind, they headed off to the barn. Rachel looked back over her shoulder at me and winked.

'That woman is a godsend,' Granna said. 'I'll be in the house.'

'I'll come help with dinner,' I said to Granna.

'I've got to go back with Simon,' Zeke said.

'I figured. But I'll see you for dinner?'

'Yes.' He waited until Granna shut the door and we were alone. 'My father called today. He wants to sell his share of the mill to Simon. Apparently, he has met a woman in San Francisco. He is going to stay there and marry her.'

'Zeke—'

'No, it's okay. Funny. I've always hated my father. Now I'm just indifferent. I don't know which is worse.'

'Neither,' I said. 'Your father is no concern of ours, at least not now. You never know. Sometime in the future, you might be able to come to an understanding and have some sort of a relationship with him.'

'See you in a couple of hours,' Zeke said. He kissed my forehead and got in the car with Simon.

* * *

Wade Connor made arrangements for our new house to be painted and readied for us to move in on the fifteenth of July. I loved the house even more by the light of day. The house was more of a cottage, really, with white shingled siding and a shale roof. It was tucked into a small street four blocks away from downtown, amid a bunch of old trees that provided ample shade. We had three bedrooms upstairs, a large living room, and an office space that Zeke and I could share. The house's best feature was the multi-paned windows in each room. I welcomed the flood of sunlight, and, with Helen's help, was busy making curtains.

179

In his neverending and oh-so-annoying efficiency, Wade had called off the FBI agents who had watched over us since we arrived in Millport. He rationalized, and Zeke agreed, that the danger we had suffered here had nothing to do with Hendrik Shrader. We had been in Millport over a month, and the FBI had not received any indication that Hendrik Shrader's long reach had extended to Zeke's hometown. Although we were relatively safe here in Millport, I realized now that I would spend my life in a heightened state of diligence, by virtue of my husband's profession. He had made enemies. I would always lock the doors to my home, and I would always be aware of my surroundings.

Daphne remained missing. Her story had faded to the back pages of the newspaper, while the front page – at least of the San Francisco papers – reported the news of the thirty-five thousand workers needed to save the July crops, and that the meat shortage was here to stay, with no hope in sight. I felt a pang of guilt at the excess of meat to be had in this part of the state, and wondered how such disparity in food distribution happened in a country such as this.

Today I was charged with going through the attic and taking whatever I needed for the new house. Granna offered to buy us furniture, but Zeke suggested that I peruse the attic first. It didn't take me long to choose two bedsteads, a dresser for Zeke, a mirror, and a set of China and silver for everyday use. Some of the dishes had cracks and chips in them, so I went through each one, unwrapping it, and sorting it, the chipped dishes in one pile, and the unchipped in another. I beavered away at this until the room started to spin, and I felt as though I were going to vomit. I stood and moved to the open window, where I sucked in fresh air and waited for the nausea to pass. I went downstairs, grabbed my purse, and headed outside, anxious to get outdoors in the sunshine.

I made it outside, despite the pounding in my head. Bright stars floated before my eyes. Another rush of nausea, this one more severe than the previous, forced me into the nearest chair. I sat for a moment, bent over with my head between my knees, taking deep breaths. When I sat up, the nausea had passed, but I still wasn't well enough to walk back to the cottage that Zeke and I now called home. I waited, focusing on the flowers and the bees. Nestled among the shrubbery were statues of griffins and gargoyles – hideous creatures. One of the odious statues leered at me, its eyes bulging, teeth bared. I shuddered.

The hair on the back of my neck stood up, just as the voice spoke behind me.

'Don't stand up.' A man's voice cut through the quiet afternoon. Cold metal pressed against the back of my head. 'You move, and I'll blow your brains out.'

'We're going in the house, and you're going to call your husband and tell him to come home.'

I started to stand up. Firm hands gripped my shoulders and pushed me back down again. 'You'll get up when I say you can get up,' the man said. I eyed my purse. It lay on the table, the gun inside. If only I could get to it.

'Okay. You can stand up. Don't turn around. Walk slowly into the house.'

I stood and grabbed my purse, stepping away from the table. I fumbled with the latch, trying to get to my gun. The man was quicker. He took the gun out of my purse, removing the bullets, which he threw into the bushes. I faced him. He was short and hatless. He had dirty brown hair that stuck to his head, either from grease that he applied or from the desperate need of a shower. His eyes traveled over my body, taking my measure from head to toe.

'You're a pretty little thing,' he said. 'You and me might have some fun.' My stomach roiled.

He stepped close and reached out his hand, as if to grab me. I flinched. Another figure, equally as filthy, stepped out from behind the Meyer Lemon bush. The figure picked up the statue of the gargoyle and struck my would-be assailant with it. The man crumpled to the ground. A pool of blood grew under his head. I stared at my protector, not quite believing what I saw.

'Daphne?'

She looked as though she hadn't eaten or slept in weeks. Her hair, usually thick and luxurious, hung in strings dark with grease. She wore men's trousers, along with a button-up shirt that might have been white at one time, but which was now a dingy gray. She swooped down and picked up the man's gun, which lay near the body. When she had it in hand, she pointed it at me.

I pushed past her to the shrubs. I vomited hot bile which burned the back of my throat. When I straightened up, Daphne was gone. She came back seconds later, the gun tucked into the waistband of her pants. She carried a glass of water which she set on the table. 'Come sit,' she said. She led me over to the chair. The smell of her triggered my gag reflex, and I prayed that I wouldn't vomit again.

'Drink that,' she said. 'Just do it slowly.'

I picked up the glass and took a few sips of water. The nausea faded away.

'Does Zeke know?' She watched me as I sipped my water.

'Where have you been?'

'Never mind that,' she said. 'I'm tired of running. At least Toby's happy. He loves that pony.'

'You've been watching him?'

'I've been under your noses this entire time. It's Toby.' A tear rolled down her cheek, clearing a trail through the grime that rested there. 'I can't leave my boy. I see Simon and Helen have finally realized their feelings for each other. I trust Helen. She'll be good to Simon and take care of Toby. Sarah, I need a favor, two favors, actually.' She laid the gun on the table between us. 'I need you to tell Sophie how sorry I am. I knew she was the Climber, and I used her horribly. I took her rucksack – on more

182

than one occasion – when I should have gotten her help. Will you tell her I'm sorry?'

'Yes,' I said. 'And the second favor?'

'Promise that no harm will come to Seadrift. I've sent a letter to the lawyer, naming you executor of my estate. I've left Seadrift to you. I hope you'll see fit to let him live in the pasture. Please promise you'll be kind.'

'I promise,' I said.

'And tell Zeke I'm sorry.'

'He knows already,' I said.

'He loves you, Sarah,' Daphne said. 'Now go and call Joe. I'm ready to turn myself in.' I got up and moved into the house, picked up the phone and had asked the operator to connect me to Joe Connor at the police station when I heard the blast of the gun.

My ears started to ring, so I couldn't really tell who answered the phone.

'Send Joe.' I hung up.

Chapter 21

Wade had insisted on paying for an actual air-conditioner in our cottage. An awkward, bulky contraption, it fit in the downstairs window and purred along all day keeping the house cool. Although I no longer heard the birds singing – the machine made a noisy whir – the relief from the heat proved a blessing. At least Wade Connor was generous with his reparations.

Two weeks had gone by since Daphne's funeral. Nick Newland's article had catapulted his career and he took a job in Washington, D.C. Zeke and I made a pact to remember the good side of Daphne – the gardener, the horsewoman, the ferocious spirit. I now understood the love that drove her over the brink of sanity into madness.

Zeke stood in the doorway between the kitchen and living room. He held a wire whisk in one hand and a bottle of cooking sherry in another. The kitchen had become his domain since we moved into our house. He spent hours concocting gourmet meals to rival the finest restaurants.

'You've got a smudge on your nose. They'll be here in fifteen minutes,' I said.

* * *

Punctual as ever, Joe, Wade, and Sophie arrived at twelve o'clock noon, on the dot. 'This air-conditioning is heavenly,' Sophie said. 'Can I move in? Or better yet, Wade, maybe I should do something heroic for you, so you can buy us an air-conditioner.'

'It really works,' Joe said. He stood in the middle of the living room, amazement written all over his face.

'Your house is gorgeous, Sarah. You really do have a nice touch,' Sophie tucked my arm in hers and surveyed the decorations and new furniture mingled in with a fair assortment from Zeke's attic.

Wade, Zeke, and Joe had moved to the air-conditioner. They stood around it, studying it, and discussing its mechanical properties. Sophie sat next to me on the settee. We stared at Rachel's portrait, which now hung over our fireplace.

'She was a wonderful person,' Sophie said.

'I feel like I know her,' I said.

Zeke and I served lunch to our first houseguests. Everyone marveled at Zeke's cooking. Wade Connor offered to finance a restaurant. When we had eaten, and I had served coffee and orange sherbet, Wade broke the silence.

'Sophie, Joe, what are your plans? Have you set a date for your wedding?'

'Next June,' Joe said. He grabbed Sophie's hand.

'What will you do, Sophie? Are you planning on going to school?'

'Not sure,' Sophie said, stuffing the last bit of sherbet into her mouth. 'I'll think of something.'

She and Wade Connor shared a look.

It was after two o'clock when everyone left. I had fallen into the habit of an afternoon nap and was ready to lie down. Zeke and I stood next to each other on the porch watching them drive away in Wade's blue car, leaving a trail of dust in their wake.

'Do you think Wade recruited Sophie to work for the FBI?' I asked.

'He might have. You don't have to sound so incredulous,

darling. She did have a successful career as a cat burglar. A skill like that might prove useful to the FBI.' We walked inside and sat down next to each other on the couch. Zeke leaned back in his seat and crossed his legs. His eyes narrowed. 'Why are you smiling?'

'I've told Dr Geisler to start looking for my replacement.'

'Why?'

'In about seven months things are going to change for both of us.' I rubbed my belly and waited for Zeke to understand what I was telling him.

'We're having a baby?' Zeke beamed. He pulled me close and kissed me.

Rachel Caen gazed down at us from over the mantle. I swear, she smiled.

The next book from Terry Lynn Thomas is coming in 2019

Turn the page for an extract from
Terry Lynn Thomas' gripping *The Silent Woman*

Prologue

Berlin, May 1936

It rained the day the Gestapo came.

Dieter Reinsinger didn't mind the rain. He liked the sound of the drops on the tight fabric of his umbrella as he walked from his office on Wilhelmstrasse to the flat he shared with his sister Leni and her husband Michael on Nollendorfstrasse. The trip took him the good part of an hour, but he walked to and from work every day, come rain or shine. He passed the familiar apartments and plazas, nodding at the familiar faces with a smile.

Dieter liked his routine. He passed Mrs Kleiman's bakery, and longed for the pfannkuchen that used to tempt passers-by from the display window. He remembered Mrs Kleiman's kind ways, as she would beckon him into the shop, where she would sit with him and share a plate of the jelly doughnuts and the strong coffee that she brewed especially to his liking. She was a kind woman, who had lost her husband and only son in the war.

In January the Reich took over the bakery, replacing gentle Mrs Kleiman with a ham-fisted fraulein with a surly attitude and no skill in the kitchen whatsoever. No use complaining over things that cannot be fixed, Dieter chided himself. He found he no longer had a taste for pfannkuchen.

By the time he turned onto his block, his sodden trouser legs clung to his calves. He didn't care. He thought of the hot coffee he would have when he got home, followed by the vegetable soup that Leni had started that morning. Dieter ignored the changes taking place around him. If he just kept to himself, he could rationalise the gangs of soldiers that patrolled the streets, taking pleasure in the fear they induced. He could ignore the lack of fresh butter, soap, sugar, and coffee. He could ignore the clenching in his belly every time he saw the pictures of Adolf Hitler, which hung in every shop, home, café, and business in Berlin. If he could carry on as usual, Dieter could convince himself that things were just as they used to be.

He turned onto his block and stopped short when he saw the black Mercedes parked at the kerb in front of his apartment. The lobby door was open. The pavement around the apartment deserted. He knew this day would come – how could it not? He just didn't know it would come so soon. The Mercedes was running, the windscreen wipers swooshing back and forth. Without thinking, Dieter shut his umbrella and tucked himself into the sheltered doorway of the apartment building across the street. He peered through the pale rain and bided his time. Soon he would be rid of Michael Blackwell. Soon he and Leni could get back to living their quiet life. Leni would thank him in the end. How could she not?

Dieter was a loyal German. He had enlisted in the Deutsches Heer – the Germany army – as an eighteen-year-old boy. He had fought in the trenches and had lived to tell about it. He came home a hardened man – grateful to still have his arms and legs attached – ready to settle down to a simple life. Dieter didn't want a wife. He didn't like women much. He didn't care much for sex, and he had Leni to care for the house. All Dieter needed was a comfortable chair at the end of the day and food for his belly. He wanted nothing else.

Leni was five years younger than Dieter. She'd celebrated her fortieth birthday in March, but to Dieter she would always be a child. While Dieter was steadfast and hardworking, Leni was wild and flighty. When she was younger she had thought she would try to be a dancer, but quickly found that she lacked the required discipline. After dancing, she turned to painting and poured her passion into her work for a year. The walls of the flat were covered with canvases filled with splatters of vivid paint. She used her considerable charm to connive a showing at a small gallery, but her work wasn't well received.

Leni claimed that no one understood her. She tossed her paint-brushes and supplies in the rubbish bin and moved on to writing. Writing was a good preoccupation for Leni. Now she called herself a writer, but rarely sat down to work. She had a desk tucked into one of the corners of the apartment, complete with a sterling fountain pen and inkwell, a gift from Dieter, who held a secret hope that his restless sister had found her calling.

Now Michael Blackwell commandeered the writing desk, the silver pen, and the damned inkwell. Just like he commandeered everything else.

For a long time, Leni kept her relationship with Michael Blackwell a secret. Dieter noticed small changes: the ink well in a different spot on Leni's writing desk and the bottle of ink actually being used. The stack of linen writing paper depleted. Had Leni started writing in earnest? Something had infused her spirit with a new effervescence. Her cheeks had a new glow to them. Leni floated around the apartment. She hummed as she cooked. Dieter assumed that his sister – like him – had discovered passion in a vocation. She bought new dresses and took special care with her appearance. When Dieter asked how she had paid for them, she told him she had been economical with the housekeeping money.

For the first time ever, the household ran smoothly. Meals were produced on time, laundry was folded and put away, and the house sparkled. Dieter should have been suspicious. He wasn't.

He discovered them in bed together on a beautiful September day when a client had cancelled an appointment and Dieter had decided to go home early. He looked forward to sitting in his chair in front of the window, while Leni brought him lunch and a stein filled with thick dark beer on a tray. These thoughts of home and hearth were in his mind when he let himself into the flat and heard the moan – soft as a heartbeat – coming from Leni's room. Thinking that she had fallen and hurt herself, Dieter burst into the bedroom, only to discover his sister naked in the bed, her limbs entwined with the long muscular legs of Michael Blackwell.

'Good God,' Michael said as he rolled off Leni and covered them both under the eiderdown. Dieter hated Michael Blackwell then, hated the way he shielded his sister, as if Leni needed protection from her own brother. Dieter bit back the scream that threatened and with great effort forced himself to unfurl his hands, which he was surprised to discover had clenched into tight fists. He swallowed the anger, taking it back into his gut where it could fester.

Leni sat up, the golden sun from the window forming a halo around her body as she held the blanket over her breasts. 'Dieter, darling,' she giggled. 'I'd like you to meet my husband.' Dieter took the giggle as a taunting insult. It sent his mind spinning. For the first time in his life, he wanted to throttle his sister.

At least Michael Blackwell had the sense to look sheepish. 'I'd shake your hand, but I'm afraid …'

'We'll explain everything,' Leni said. 'Let us get dressed. Michael said he'd treat us to a special dinner. We must celebrate!'

Dieter had turned on his heel and left the flat. He didn't return until late that evening, expecting Leni to be alone, hurt, or even angry with him. He expected her to come running to the door

194

when he let himself in and beg his forgiveness. But Leni wasn't alone. She and Michael were waiting for Dieter, sitting on the couch. Leni pouted. Michael insisted the three of them talk it out and come to an understanding. 'Your sister loves you, Dieter. Don't make her choose between us.'

Michael took charge – as he was wont to do. Leni explained that she loved Michael, and that they had been seeing each other for months, right under Dieter's nose. Dieter imagined the two of them, naked, loving each other, while he slaved at the office to put food on the table.

'You could have told me, Leni,' he said to his sister. 'I've never kept anything from you.'

'You would have forbidden me to see him,' Leni said. She had taken Michael's hand. 'And I would have defied you.'

She was right. He would have forbidden the relationship. As for Leni's defiance, Dieter could forgive his foolish sister that trespass. Michael Blackwell would pay the penance for Leni's sins. After all, he was to blame for them.

Leni left them to discuss the situation man to man. Dieter found himself telling Michael about their parents' deaths and the life he and Leni shared. Michael told Dieter that he was a journalist in England and was in Germany to research a book. So that's where the ink and paper have been going, Dieter thought. When he realised that for the past few months Michael and Leni had been spending their days here, in the flat that he paid for, Dieter hated Michael Blackwell even more. But he didn't show it.

Michael brought out a fine bottle of brandy. The two men stayed up all night, talking about their lives, plans for the future, and the ever-looming war. When the sun crept up in the morning sky, they stood and shook hands. Dieter decided he could pretend to like this man. He'd do it for Leni's sake.

'I love your sister, Dieter. I hope to be friends with you,' Michael said.

Dieter wanted to slap him. Instead he forced a smile. 'I'm happy for you.'

'Do you mind if we stay here until we find a flat of our own?'

'Of course. Why move? I'd be happy if you both would live here in the house. I'll give you my bedroom. It's bigger and has a better view. I'm never home anyway.'

Michael nodded. 'I'd pay our share, of course. I'll discuss it with Leni.'

Leni agreed to stay in the flat, happy that her new husband and her brother had become friends.

Months went by. The three of them fell into a routine. Each morning, Leni would make both men breakfast. They would sit together and share a meal, after which Dieter would leave for the office. Dieter had no idea what Michael Blackwell got up to during the day. Michael didn't discuss his personal activities with Dieter. Dieter didn't ask about them.

He spent more and more time in his room after dinner, leaving Leni and Michael in the living room of the flat. He told himself he didn't care, until he noticed subtle changes taking place. They would talk in whispers, but when Dieter entered the room, they stopped speaking and stared at him with blank smiles on their faces.

It was about this time when Dieter noticed a change in his neighbours. They used to look at him and smile. Now they wouldn't look him in the eye, and some had taken to crossing the street when he came near. They no longer stopped to ask after his health or discuss the utter lack of decent coffee or meat. His neighbours were afraid of him. Leni and Michael were up to something, or Michael was up to something and Leni was blindly following along.

During this time, Dieter noticed a man milling outside the flat when he left for his walk to the office. He recognised him, as he had been there the day before, standing in the doorway in the apartment building across the street. Fear clenched Dieter's gut, cramping his bowels. He forced himself to breathe, to keep his eyes focused straight ahead and continue on as though nothing were amiss. He knew a Gestapo agent when he saw one. He heard the rumours of Hitler's secret police. Dieter was a good German. He kept his eyes on the ground and his mouth shut.

Once he arrived at his office, he hurried up to his desk and peered out the window onto the street below. Nothing. So they weren't following him. Of course they weren't following him. Why would they? It didn't take Dieter long to figure out that Michael Blackwell had aroused the Gestapo's interest. He had to protect Leni. He vowed to find out what Michael was up to.

His opportunity came on a Saturday in April, when Leni and Michael had plans to be out for the day. They claimed they were going on a picnic, but Dieter was certain they were lying when he discovered the picnic hamper on the shelf in the kitchen. He wasn't surprised. His sister was a liar now. It wasn't her fault. He blamed Michael Blackwell. He had smiled and wished them a pleasant day. After that, he moved to the window and waited until they exited the apartment, arm in arm, and headed away on their outing. When they were safely out of sight, Dieter bolted the door and conducted a thorough, methodical search.

He went through all of the books in the flat, thumbing through them before putting them back exactly as he found them. Nothing. He rifled drawers, looked under mattresses, went through pockets. Still nothing. Desperate now, he removed everything from the wardrobe where Michael and Leni hung their clothes. Only after everything was removed did Dieter see the wooden crate on the floor, tucked into the back behind Michael's tennis racket. He took it out and lifted the lid, to reveal neat stacks of brochures, the front of which depicted a castle and a charming German village. The cover read, Lernen Sie Das Schone Deutschland: Learn About Beautiful Germany. Puzzled, Dieter took one of the brochures, opened it, read the first sentence, and cried out.

Inside the brochure was a detailed narrative of the conditions under Hitler's regime. The writer didn't hold back. The brochure told of an alleged terror campaign of murder, mass arrests, execution, and an utter suspension of civil rights. There was a map of all the camps, which – at least according to this brochure – held over one hundred thousand or more Communists, Social Democrats, and trade unionists. The last page was a plea for help, a battle cry calling for Hitler and his entire regime to be overthrown.

Dieter's hand shook. Fear made his mouth go dry. They would all be taken to the basement at Prinz Albrecht Strasse for interrogation and torture. If they survived, they would be sent to one of the camps. A bullet to the back of the head would be a mercy. Sweat broke out on Dieter's face; drops of it formed between his shoulder blades. He swallowed the lump that formed in the back of his throat, as the fear morphed into blind, infuriating anger and exploded in a black cloud of rage directed at Michael Blackwell.

How dare he expose Leni to this type of danger? Dieter needed to protect his sister. He stuffed the brochures back in the crate, put the lid on it, and pushed the box back into the recesses of the wardrobe. There was only one thing for Dieter to do.

Chapter 1

Marry in haste, repent at leisure, says the bird in the gilded cage.
The words – an apt autobiography to be sure – ran round and
round in Cat Carlisle's head. She pressed her forehead against
the cold windowpane and scanned the street in front of her house.
Her eyes roamed the square, with its newly painted benches and
gnarled old trees leafed out in verdant June splendour. A gang
of school-aged boys kicked a ball on the grass, going out of their
way to push and shove as they scurried along. They laughed with
glee when the tallest of the group fell on his bum, turned a
somersault, popped back up, and bowed deeply to his friends.
She smiled and pushed away the longing that threatened when-
ever a child was near.

She thought of the time when she and her husband had loved
each other, confided in each other. How long had it been since
they'd had a civil conversation? Five years? Ten? How long had
it been since she discovered that Benton Carlisle and Trudy
Ashworth – of the Ashworth textile fortune – were involved in a
long-term love affair? Ten years, two months and four days. For
the record book, that's how long it took for Benton's love to
morph into indifference and for the indifference to fester into
acrimony. Now Cat and her husband rarely spoke. On the rare

occasions when they did speak, the words between them were sharp and laced with animosity.

Cat turned and surveyed the room that she had claimed for her own, a small sanctuary in the Carlisles' Kensington house. When she and Benton discovered she was with child the first time, they pulled down the gloomy wallpaper and washed the walls a charming shade of buttercup yellow, perfect for a child of any sex. But Cat had lost the child before the furniture had been ordered. In an abundance of caution, they hadn't ordered furniture when Cat became pregnant for a second and third time. Those babies had not survived in her womb either. Now she had claimed the nursery as her own.

It was the sunniest room in the house. When Benton started to stay at his club – at least that's what he told Cat; she knew he really stayed at Trudy's flat in Belgravia – Cat moved in and decorated it to suit her own taste. She found she rather liked this small space. A tiny bed, an armoire to hold her clothes, and a writing table – with space between the pieces – were the only furnishings in the room. She had removed the dark Persian rug and left the oak floors bare, liking the way the honey-toned wood warmed the room. She had washed away the buttercup yellow and painted the walls stark white.

'Miss?' The maid stood in the open doorway of Cat's bedroom. She was too young to be working, thirteen if she was a day, skinny and pale with a mousy brown bun peeking out from the white cap and sharp cheekbones that spoke of meals missed.

'Who're you?' Cat asked. She forced a smile so as not to scare the poor thing.

'Annie, ma'am.' Annie took a tentative step into Cat's room. In one hand she carried a wooden box full of feather dusters, rags, and other cleaning supplies. In the other she carried a broom and dustpan. 'I'm to give you the message that Alicia Montrose is here. She is eager to see you.' She looked around the room. 'And then I am to turn your room.'

200

'I'll just finish up and be down shortly,' Cat said.

The girl hesitated in the doorway.

'You can come in and get started,' Cat said.

'Thank you, miss.' The girl moved into the room and started to work away, focusing on the tasks at hand. 'Do you mind if I open the window? I like to air the bed linens.'

'Of course not,' Cat said.

She reached for the box that held her hairpins and attempted to wrangle her curls into submission. Behind her, the child opened the window and pulled back the sheets on Cat's bed. While the bed linens aired, Annie busied herself with the dusting and polishing.

Cat turned back to the mirror and wondered how she could avoid seeing Alicia Montrose. She couldn't face her, not yet. The wounds, though old, were still raw.

The Montrose family had always been gracious and kind to her, especially in the beginning of her relationship with Benton when she felt like a fish out of water, among the well-heeled, tightly knit group who had known each other since childhood, and whose parents and grandparents before them had been close friends.

Many in Benton's circle hadn't been so quick to welcome Cat into their fold. Not the Montroses. They extended every courtesy towards Cat. Alicia took Cat under her wing and saw that she was included in the events the wives scheduled when the husbands went on their hunting and fishing trips. Alicia also sought Cat out for days of shopping and attending the museum. And when the Bradbury-Scots invited Cat and Benton for dinner, Alicia swept in and tactfully explained the myriad of customs involved.

'They'll be watching you, Cat. If you hold your teacup incorrectly, they'll never let you live it down. And Lady Bradbury-Scott will load the table with an excess of forks and knives just to trip you up.' Alicia had taken Cat to her home every day for a week, where they dined on course after course of delicious food prepared by the Montroses' cook. While they ate, Alicia explained every nuance to Cat – *speak to the guest on the right during the first course. Only when that is finished can you turn to the left.* The rules were legion.

Cat credited Alicia's tutelage for her success at the dinner. She had triumphed. The Bradbury-Scotts accepted her, so did Benton's friends, all thanks to Alicia Montrose. One of these days Cat would need to make peace with Alicia, and talk to her about why she had resisted Alicia's overtures. Cat didn't expect Alicia to forgive her. How could she? But at least Alicia could be made to understand what motivated Cat to behave so shabbily. But not today.

She plunked her new green velvet hat on her head and pinned it fast without checking herself in the mirror. As she tiptoed downstairs, she wondered if she could sneak out the kitchen door and avoid the women altogether. With any luck, she could slip out unnoticed and avoid the litany of questions and criticisms that had become Isobel's standard fare over the years.

'I think the chairs should be in a half circle around this half of the room.' Alicia's voice floated up the stairs. 'A half circle is so much more welcoming, don't you agree?'

'Oh, I agree.' Isobel Carlisle, Cat's domineering sister-in-law, a shrewish woman who made a career of haranguing Cat, spoke in the unctuous tone reserved for Alicia alone. 'Move them back, Marie.'

Poor Marie. Isobel's secretary bore the brunt of Isobel's self-importance. Cat didn't know how she stood it, but Marie Quimby had been Isobel's loyal servant for years. Cat slunk down the stairs like a thief in her own home.

'But we just had them in the half circle, and neither of you liked that arrangement,' Marie said. She sounded beleaguered and it was only nine in the morning.

'There you are, Catherine. Bit late this morning.' Isobel stepped into the hallway.'

Catherine,' Alicia said. She smiled as she air-kissed Cat's cheek, while Isobel looked down her nose in disapproval. 'How've you been, Cat? You're looking well. We were worried about you. Good to see you've got the roses back in your cheeks.' Alicia was resplendent in a navy dress and a perfect hat.

'It was just a bout of influenza. I am fully recovered,' Cat said. 'And thank you for the lovely flowers and the card.'

'Won't you consider helping us? We could certainly use you. No one has a knack for getting people to part with their money like you do.'

Cat smiled, ignoring Isobel's dagger-like glare. 'Maybe next time. How're the boys?'

'Growing like mad. Hungry all the time. They're excited about our trip to Scotland. The invitation's open, if you'd like to join?' Alicia let the question hang in the air between them.

'I'll think about it.' Cat backed out of the room, eager to be outside. 'It's good to see you, Alicia.'

'Come to the house for the weekend, Cat. If the boys are too much, I'll send them to their gran's house. We've some catching up to do.'

'I'd like that,' Cat said. 'Must run.'

'Perhaps we should get back to work?' Isobel said.

A flash of sadness washed over Alicia's face. 'Please ring me, Catherine. At least we can have lunch.'

'I will. Promise,' Cat said.

'Isobel, I'll leave you to deal with the chairs. I'm going to use your telephone and call the florist.'

'Of course,' Isobel said.

Once Alicia stepped away, Isobel stepped close to Cat and spoke in a low voice. 'I do not appreciate you being so forward. You practically threw yourself at Alicia. Don't you realise what my association on this project could do for me, for our family, socially? This is very important, Catherine. Don't force me to speak to Benton about your behaviour. I will if I have to.'

Cat ignored her sister-in-law, as she had done a million times before. She walked past the drawing room, where Marie was busy arranging the chairs – heavy wooden things with curvy legs and high backs. Marie looked up at Cat and gave her a wan smile.

Isobel, stout and strong with a mass of iron-grey waves, was the exact opposite of Marie, who was thin as a cadaver and obedient as a well-trained hound. Marie's wispy grey hair stood in a frizzy puff on her head, like a mangled halo. Cat didn't understand the relationship between the women. Isobel claimed that her volunteer work kept her so busy that she needed an assistant to make her appointments and type her letters. Cat didn't believe that for one minute. Cat knew the true reason for Marie's employment. Isobel needed someone to boss around.

Her sister-in-law surveyed Cat's ensemble from head to toe, looking for fault. Cat dismissed her scrutiny. After fifteen years of living in the Carlisle house, she had become a master at disregarding Isobel.

'What is it, Isobel? I really must go,' Cat said.

'Before you go, I'd like you to touch up the silver. And maybe you could give Marie a hand in the kitchen? I know it's a bit of an imposition, but the agency didn't have a cook available today. I'm expecting ten committee members for our meeting this afternoon. I wouldn't want to run out of food. I need these committee members well fed. We've much work to do.'

'I can manage, Izzy,' Marie said.

'I've asked Catherine,' Isobel said. 'And those chairs won't move themselves.'

'I'm going out.' Cat paused before the mirror. She fixed her hat and fussed with her hair, taking her time as she drew the delicate veil over her eyes.

'You should be grateful, Catherine. Benton has given you a home and a position in society. You've made it clear you're not happy here, but a little gratitude wouldn't go amiss. You and Benton may be at odds, but that doesn't change things. You'd be on the street if it weren't for us. You've no training. It's not like you are capable of earning your living.'

'I hardly think any gratitude I feel towards my husband should be used to benefit you. I'm not your servant, Isobel. I'm Benton's wife. You seem to have forgotten that.'

Isobel stepped so close to Cat that their noses almost touched. When she spoke, spittle flew, but Cat didn't flinch. She didn't back away when Isobel said, 'I suggest you take care in your deal- ings with me, Catherine. I could ruin you.'

Cat met Isobel's gaze and didn't look away. 'Do your best. I am not afraid of you.' She stepped away and forced a smile. 'Silly old cow,' Cat whispered.

'What did you call me?'

'You heard me.' Cat picked up her handbag. 'I don't know when I'll be back. Have a pleasant day.' She turned her back on Isobel and stepped out into the summer morning.

She headed out into the street and took one last glance at the gleaming white house, one of many in a row. Benton's cousin, Michael Blackwell, Blackie for short, stood in the window of Benton's study, bleary-eyed from a night of solitary drinking in his room. Blackie spent a lot of time in Benton's study, especially when Benton wasn't home. She knew why – that's where the good brandy was kept.

Blackie had escaped Germany with his life, the clothes on his back, and nothing else. A long-lost cousin of Benton and Isobel, Blackie turned up on their doorstep, damaged from the narrow escape and desperate for a place to live. Of course they had taken him in. The Carlisles were big on family loyalty. Now Blackie worked at a camera shop during the day and spent his nights sequestered in his room with a bottle of brandy and his memo- ries of Hitler.

Cat often wondered what happened in Germany to frighten Blackie so, but she didn't have the heart to make him relive his suffering just to satisfy her curiosity. He saw Cat, smiled at her, and held up a snifter of Benton's brandy, never mind that it was only half past nine in the morning. Everyone knew Blackie drank to excess. They didn't care. He was family. Cat waved at him, anxious to get as far away from the Carlisle house as fast as she could.

Dear Reader,

Thank you so much for taking the time to read this book – we hope you enjoyed it! If you did, we'd be so appreciative if you left a review.

Here at HQ Digital we are dedicated to publishing fiction that will keep you turning the pages into the early hours. We publish a variety of genres, from heartwarming romance, to thrilling crime and sweeping historical fiction.

To find out more about our books, enter competitions and discover exclusive content, please join our community of readers by following us at:

🖸 *@HQDigitalUK*

🄵 *facebook.com/HQDigitalUK*

Are you a budding writer? We're also looking for authors to join the HQ Digital family! Please submit your manuscript to:

HQDigital@harpercollins.co.uk.

Hope to hear from you soon!

DIGITAL
HQ

If you enjoyed *The Drowned Woman*, then why not try another spine-tingling read from HQ Digital?